"Thank you, Cooper. You've been wonderful."

Lauren's eyes flashed, all that meadow green working magic on him. Holding her like this felt right, and that was all wrong. But when she dipped her gaze to his mouth, the longing in her eyes did him in.

"Cooper."

He put his hands in her hair and tilted her head up. Their eyes locked, wrecking his resistance, wrecking any semblance of rational thought. He brought his mouth down and touched his lips to hers. It was Fourth of July fireworks and sweet cake on Sunday morning all rolled up into one. She was soft and delicate and amazingly sexy. But one brush of the lips wasn't enough; he needed more, demanded more. She made little noises in the back of her throat, and the sounds were like music and laughter and brightness. His body grew tight and hard, and Lauren was just as lost, just as needy. She hugged his neck, ran her fingers through his hair and he deepened the kiss even more.

* * *

The Texan's Wedding Escape is part of the Heart of Stone duet from *USA TODAY* bestselling author Charlene Sands

Dear Reader,

What does a Texan do when he's asked to accomplish the near impossible?

He takes on the challenge.

In this case, my hero, Cooper Stone, has no choice. His best friend's momma believes with all of her heart that her daughter, Lauren Abbott, is about to make a huge mistake—and marry a man who is all wrong for her. Unfortunately, Cooper can't disagree. He's done some digging into her fiancé's financial doings, and what he's learned would have his best friend going ballistic, if only Tony were still on this earth.

Now Cooper has the monumental task of stopping Lauren's wedding. At all costs.

But what Coop never figured on was the heartbreaking cost he would have to pay. The sacrifice is almost too much to bear, but his sense of honor has him going through with his plan. Until Lauren turns the tables on him and tilts his world completely upside down. My heroines tend to do that! Take the journey with Cooper and Lauren, and I hope with all my heart you enjoy the ride.

Happy reading, my friends,

Charlene Sands

(And be sure to look for Jared Stone's story coming later this year!)

CHARLENE SANDS

——

THE TEXAN'S WEDDING ESCAPE

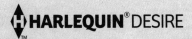

Recycling programs
for this product may
not exist in your area.

ISBN-13: 978-1-335-97145-6

The Texan's Wedding Escape

HARLEQUIN®
www.Harlequin.com

Printed in U.S.A.

Charlene Sands is a *USA TODAY* bestselling author of more than forty romance novels. She writes sensual contemporary romances and stories of the Old West. When not writing, Charlene enjoys sunny Pacific beaches, great coffee, reading books from her favorite authors and spending time with her family. You can find her on Facebook and Twitter, write her at PO Box 4883, West Hills, CA 91308 or sign up for her newsletter for fun blogs and ongoing contests at charlenesands.com.

Visit her Author Profile page at Harlequin.com, or charlenesands.com, for more titles.

This book is dedicated to my friends and terrific authors Leanne Banks, Lynne Marshall and Robin Bielman, who all had a hand in helping me plot the delicate balance of this story.

I love you all to pieces!

One

He hit Delete on his laptop, wiping out names and phone numbers of the women he'd dated, wanted to date or just plain thought were freaking gorgeous. Instantly, Cooper Stone's fun-loving, party-till-you-drop days were over, ended by a finger stroke on the keyboard. It was equivalent to burning his little black book, only nobody carried a little black book anymore. Things had gotten too damn sophisticated, but the end result was the same. Cooper Stone was out of the running. It was a long time coming, six months to be exact.

He wouldn't miss those names.

Not like he missed his buddy, Tony Abbott.

One minute he was laughing alongside him in the car, their heads thrown back, enjoying life to the fullest, and the next, he was silenced by the stony sound of death. The quiet in that moment still rang in Cooper's head, still tormented him. Everything had stopped, everything had gone numbingly cold. Tony had died instantly and the drunken driver behind the wheel of the car that had plowed into them had escaped without injury. So had Cooper. And he'd never forgiven himself for that.

Deleting those names was only a formality. He hadn't been a party animal since that night. And he never would be again. Some things just left a mark and the imprint of that horrible crash brought him full circle. He now lived quietly on his ranch at Stone Ridge and poured himself into his entrepreneurial businesses.

"Hey, Coop, you need some company today? I'm willing to drive out with you."

"Thanks, bro. But you don't have to do that. I've got this."

Cooper rose from his desk in the study and put on a lightweight tan jacket. It was late spring, the sunshine giving way to gray clouds that were moving in fast. Texas weather could never be counted on and it was fitting, he supposed, that this day was as glum as his mood. These bad-weather days made it easy for him to stay inside and work, giving him an excuse not to visit friends or to go to parties. Ole Coop wasn't fun anymore. And that was fine with him.

"I'll be back in a few hours."

His brother, Jared, slapped him on the back but had a look of concern on his face. "Take care and I'll see you later, okay?" That was code for "Drive safely and I love you." Jared was his baby brother who, at twenty-eight, wasn't such a baby anymore. But he worried. Just about everyone worried about him. "Okay."

It took Cooper five minutes to drive off Stone land on the outskirts of Dallas and another twenty to get to the suburb of Providence. He made a stop at the bakery and as soon as the woman behind the counter spotted him, she said, "A dozen raspberry-jelly doughnuts coming right up."

He gave her a nod. "Thank you kindly."

And within a few minutes Cooper was back on the road, the bakery box on the passenger seat beside him. He drove down the highway, leaving Providence in the dust, and eventually arrived at the Eternal Peace cemetery. When he turned into the driveway, passing a new grave covered by a hill of fresh flowers, a punch of pain attacked his stomach. A fresh grave meant loss. People were hurting: fathers, mothers, sisters, brothers, wives and children. He'd never given mortality much thought until Tony died in the prime of his life.

Cooper drove on until he reached the gravesite nestled under a tall oak. He parked the car, took a deep breath and got out. With box in hand and head down, he made his way over to Tony's resting place. The wind kicked up, the air chilly as he began speaking.

"Hi, Tone. It's me again. Been a month. Got you your favorite doughnuts." He sat on perfectly mowed grass. "You remember, the ones we never did get to eat t-that night."

He opened the box and took out one of the powdery confections. "They're your favorite, pal." He bit into it and chewed. One bite was all he could ever muster before putting the doughnut back in the box. "Wow. That was good."

At the sound of leaves crunching behind him, he turned around. It was Loretta Abbott, Tony's mother. Cooper rose immediately. "Hello, Loretta."

"Am I interrupting?"

"Gosh, no. Just having a little chat with Tony." He didn't know what else to say.

She gave him a sad smile. "You're a wonderful friend."

He wasn't. He was alive and Tony was gone. Cooper should've seen that car coming. He should've been more alert. Instead of relaxing at the wheel, joking with his friend, getting him killed.

He strode over to her and put out his arms. She walked into them and they embraced. "I'm glad to see you," she whispered.

He nodded. "Same here."

"I knew you'd be here. That's why I've come."

He backed away enough to really look at her. "Did you want to talk to me?"

She nodded, tears filling her eyes. "Yes. I'm sorry for interrupting, but I knew you'd be here on the anniversary of my Tony's accident."

He took a big swallow. "You could've called me or come to the house. You know you're welcome anytime."

The wind howled, blowing her soft brown hair out of the knot at the top of her head. "I'm afraid, I wouldn't have had the nerve to come. But something drew me here today. Somehow this way, it wouldn't be too hard to ask you what I'm about to ask you. I'm sorry to say, I'm a bit desperate and I need a favor."

"Of course. Anything. I told you if you ever needed anything to come to me."

Another sad smile graced Loretta's face. "I'm counting on that. It's about Lauren."

Tony's younger sister? She'd been working in Dallas, following in the footsteps of her mother as a nurse. Cooper hadn't seen much of her until the funeral.

Back in the day, when he and Tony were kids, they'd played travel football together for the Texas Tridents. Their friendship had only grown over the years. Often they'd spend time at each other's houses for days on end and throughout the summer months. As they got older whenever Loretta'd had to take a double shift at the hospital, he and Tony would watch Lauren until Mrs. Abbott got home. Seemed like eons ago. "What about Lauren?"

"She just got engaged to Roger Kelsey on a whim and it's all so terribly wrong. Now, she's planning to get married in less than a month. All because Roger's putting pressure on her." Loretta wiped at her tears with a tissue. "What's wrong with my girl waiting a little longer, to make sure of her feelings? We've all had a terrible shock when we lost Tony, and Lauren getting engaged—to Tony's business partner, no less—makes no sense. Roger never paid any attention to her while Tony was alive, but as soon as my son dies, he turns on the charm and proposes marriage?

"Lauren thinks she knows best, and she won't listen to me on this. She says I'm being overprotective. It doesn't add up, Cooper. Not at all."

Cooper didn't like what he was hearing. Normally he'd chalk Lauren's engagement up to falling hard when you're at your most vulnerable. After all, this happened immediately after Tony's death. Granted, some people married after only knowing each other a few weeks and found marital bliss that way but not that often.

But Lauren marrying Roger Kelsey?

Roger was a charmer and a playboy who went through women with the stealth of a panther. Tony would have seen red and never approved.

A deep sigh rose from Cooper's chest. One of the last conversations he'd had with Tony pounded in his head.

"I think Kelsey's siphoning money from my profits. Things aren't adding up," Tony had said. "I don't have solid proof yet, but I'm working on it. If my suspicions are correct, he's breaking the law and cheating me blind." Tony had vowed to get to the bottom of it.

Cooper faced Loretta, certain now he had to intervene. Not only for Loretta and Lauren, but because Tony would've wanted him to. "I'm sorry, but what can I do? Just name it."

"Oh, Cooper, I was hoping you would say that," she said, relieved. Her face relaxed and she looked at him with the tiniest hint of a smile. He was glad he could comfort her. There wasn't anything he wouldn't do to help Tony's mother.

"I need you to stop the wedding."

* * *

As soon as her mama opened the front door and Cooper walked in, something warm and fuzzy ran through Lauren's veins. At twenty-six, she thought she'd be over her fascination. But that rugged face, that sharp profile, the amazing sky blue in his eyes—all spoke of happy times during her childhood when the boys, Tony and Cooper, would include her in their antics. She'd loved being with them, even if they were both six years older and dreadfully overprotective of her.

When she'd turned twelve, barely old enough to understand crazy, out-of-whack hormones, she'd developed the worst crush on Cooper Stone. It had lasted two long and lean years until she'd graduated middle school. Then, in high school, she'd fallen hopelessly in love with Brendan Marsh. Her crush on Brendan ended after five weeks when she'd discovered Toby Strickland, Providence High's premiere quarterback. Shortly after, there was Gregory Bell, pitcher for the Providence High Pirates.

Her list of crushes was long. She was forever falling in and out of love. Katy, her bestie, and the rest of her friends would tease her, saying she wasn't a flake, just a hopeless romantic. But she'd matured while in college. She'd only fallen for one boy at UCLA. Unfortunately he wasn't the One and as soon as they'd come to that mutual conclusion, they'd parted ways.

This time, her love for Roger was the real deal. He'd been there for her during that trying, heartbreaking time right after Tony passed away. He'd been her rock.

Her support. Lord knows she'd needed that so much during that time. Roger had made her laugh and given her hope. And they'd cried together, comforted each other.

She knew it deep down in her heart. He was Tony's partner, friend and a wonderful man. How could she not love him?

Yet tonight, seeing Cooper in her mother's house brought a measure of familiarity and comfort. She had a favor to ask him and she hoped it wasn't asking too much. "I'm so glad you came for dinner," she said, walking over to him.

He put out his arms and she flowed into them. Being in his strong embrace cushioned her heart and made her feel closer to the brother she'd lost. Cooper had blamed himself for the accident, but everyone knew it hadn't been his fault. He hadn't been the one drinking and driving. He couldn't possibly have known the other driver was going to career off his side of the road and slam into them. So hugging Cooper was a way for her to comfort him, too. A way to tell him she didn't hold him responsible for her brother's death.

"I'm glad, too, Laurie Loo."

She chuckled. "You haven't called me that for at least a decade."

"Yeah, I know. You used to hate it."

"I'll let you in on my secret. I only pretended to hate it." She'd actually thought his nickname for her was kind of sweet. It was the way he'd say it, with deep affection rather than mockery, that kept her crush for him alive.

"Come in, Cooper," her mother said. "Dinner's almost ready. Why don't you and Lauren have a seat in the family room while I go check on things?"

"You need a hand, Loretta?" Cooper asked.

"No, no, no. You two go on and catch up. I'll be fine," she said, stepping out of the room.

"Mama likes doing it all herself. That's never going to change. Even though she retired from nursing, she can't seem to keep still. I suppose it's a good thing." Except when she was meddling in her life.

Her mother meant well, but her irrational arguments against her marrying Roger weren't fair. Yes, her mama married her father after dating only two months and, yes, their marriage had gotten off to a rocky start. But Mama hadn't really known him, not the way Lauren knew Roger. David Abbott'd had a wandering eye and her mother had been too blinded by love not to see it. Until her father had picked up and left his family.

Before he'd died, he'd been married and divorced three other times. So, of course, her mother would think that Lauren wasn't thinking this through. Sadly, her mother had scars that hadn't healed and she didn't want her only daughter to end up that way too. And that was part of the reason Lauren needed to see Cooper. For backup. Her mama trusted Cooper. If he could give her the approval she needed, she was sure her mama would back off.

Cooper nodded. "No doubt. Keeping busy is healthy for the soul."

"Well, then, Mama's soul is in ridiculously good shape."

Lauren led him to the brushed-suede sofa in the family room and gestured for him to sit. The cushions sank a bit as they both took a seat. Lauren crossing her legs and garnering an appreciative look from Cooper. She'd dressed up for the occasion, a soft, cocoa, lacy dress and heels, a far cry from the scrubs she usually wore. Suddenly her nerves started bouncing like a Ping-Pong ball. This was an important night. She needed an ally.

Cooper gave her a megawatt smile. "You look great. How've you been?"

"I am great," she said. "I have news and I wanted to share it with you right away."

"Okay," he said, leaning back against the sofa, giving her his full attention. "Sounds important."

She put out her left hand and her square-cut, two-carat diamond ring sparkled under his nose. "I'm engaged to Roger Kelsey. Isn't it wonderful?"

Cooper held her hand to peer at the ring on her finger. A little zing flittered through her system. She may not have completely gotten over her little crush on him from ages ago, but that wasn't love or anything close. Nope, Cooper was a dear family friend and...well, he was like a big brother to her.

"What it is," he said, his eyes softening to hers, "is a little sudden, isn't it, Lauren?"

"I know, Cooper. Mama said the same thing, but she doesn't know how glorious Roger makes me feel. So what if we haven't been dating long. They say, when it's right, it's right."

"Who's 'they'?" he asked.

She gave her head a tilt. Not Cooper, too. Her mama

hadn't been overjoyed about her quick engagement and now Cooper, Tony's brother from another mother, was giving her a hard time. "You're big-brothering me again."

"Tony's not here to do it."

"I know." She put her head down. It hurt terribly to think Tony wasn't going to be at her wedding. They'd been close all their lives, until that fateful accident. "It's not that I don't appreciate it, Cooper. I know you're just looking out for my welfare, but this time, I've got it."

"Got what?"

"*It.* You know, love, marriage, everything that goes with it. It's under control and time for me to settle down. I'm twenty-six years old and I want more out of life. The one thing Tony's death taught me is to not take life for granted. I'm ready, Cooper."

His gaze roamed over her face as she waited breathlessly for his approval. More than anything, she wanted his blessing. Finally his lips parted in a small, encouraging smile. "Okay. Well, then, I'm happy for you."

"Oh, Cooper. Thank you!" She lunged for him and squeezed his neck, hugging him tight. Whiffs of his manly cologne surrounded her, but she was too happy to dwell on how much that appealed to her. "This means so much to me…you'll never know." Tears welled in her eyes. She had his blessing. It would be easier for her mama to accept her marriage to Roger now. "There's one thing, though…a favor I need to ask you. You're not like family to us, you *are* family, and…well, since my dad is gone, and now Tony, too, I was hoping that on my wedding day, you'd do me the honor of walking me down the aisle."

* * *

Cooper paced inside Loretta's kitchen. He'd come in here the second Lauren had excused herself to take a phone call and now he was realizing how hard this mission would be. If he spoke negatively about Kelsey without any proof of his bad intentions, Lauren would shut him down. He'd seen it happen before. Lauren was strong-willed, stubborn and independent. Through the years, Tony had learned how to rein her in. He'd gained her trust and had actually gotten her to listen to him at times. But he wasn't Tony. Cooper only had a brother and was the first to admit he had no skills understanding the female mind. Not when it came to stopping a young woman from possibly making a big mistake.

A little voice in his head told him to back off and let Lauren find out about Kelsey on her own. A leopard always revealed his spots…or some such notion. But Lauren had been hurt enough and so had Loretta, for that matter. He'd given Tony's mother his word.

Loretta was busy putting hot rolls into a lined basket. He pulled the aroma into his nostrils, but the garlicky cheese scent did nothing to whet his appetite.

"Say what's on your mind," the older woman said quietly.

Cooper ran a hand down his face. "Loretta, she's asked me to walk her down the aisle. Man, that puts me in a difficult spot. Lauren is so damn happy."

"What did you say to her?"

"What could I say? I couldn't hurt her. I told her it would be my honor to take Tony's place by her side."

The hand Loretta put on his shoulder was warm and

comforting. "She doesn't know her own heart, Cooper. Trust me on this. She's thought herself in love half a dozen times in her lifetime. Kelsey is not the man for her. You won't hurt her, but he will."

He hadn't told a soul about Tony's suspicions about his partner cheating him, but maybe now was the time to broach the subject. "Loretta, what's going on at Kelsey-Abbott? How often do you go into the office?"

"Me? I've been a nurse for thirty-five years. What do I know about real-estate development? I told my Tony years ago not to include me in his will. I'm comfortable and have everything I need."

"So, you're saying that Tony's half of the company—"

"Goes to Lauren. Yes, that's the way we'd agreed."

Cooper stared at her. Soon, Loretta's eyes began blinking almost as fast as his mind was spinning. "Oh, dear. You don't think that he's marrying her to gain control of the entire company, do you?"

It wasn't unheard of and, in fact, the more he thought about it, the more it made sense. If Roger Kelsey was married to Lauren, there would be no need for anyone to check over the books, to reframe the partnership, to find out he'd been cheating Tony. It was likely that Lauren wouldn't want to get involved in the company at all, not if her new husband had everything under control. She was as dedicated to nursing as her mother had been. "Could be, Loretta," he murmured.

"Hey!" Lauren came bounding into the room, a big smile on her face. "There you are. I was wondering what happened to you, Cooper. And my ears are burning. Were you both talking about me?"

"Yep, as a matter of fact we were," Cooper said, giving Loretta a glance. "You told me you haven't picked a venue for the wedding yet."

"Yes, that's right. We're going to do something simple."

"But, honey, you've always dreamed of a big wedding," Loretta interjected, disapproval clouding her soft brown eyes. "That's the least Roger can do for you."

"I know, Mama. But there isn't time for that and I'm fine…with it." The disappointment on her face told a different story.

"You shouldn't be fine with anything. You should be ecstatic. We're talking about your wedding day, honey."

"Problem solved," Cooper announced and two curious female gazes landed on him.

He hoped like hell he wasn't making a whopper of a mistake, but the idea taking shape in his mind wasn't anything short of brilliant. What he needed was time with Lauren to make sure she wasn't getting in over her head and marrying this guy impulsively. Which seemed likely. Tony hadn't trusted him, Loretta thought she was being rash and now Cooper was smack-dab in the middle of it all. Keeping Lauren close—and away from Roger—was key. There was only one way he figured he could pull that off.

"You're getting married at my ranch at Stone Ridge. I insist. You'll speak your vows at my home. I'll open the place up to you and you can come and stay with me while you make your plans. Heck, both you and your mama are welcome to stay on the ranch. The two of you can work together and, Lauren, you'll have the wedding you've always dreamed about. I promise not to get in your way."

A promise he would probably have to break because he planned on protecting Lauren from being hurt no matter what.

Lauren's pretty, pale green eyes brightened. She opened her mouth to say something but after a split second, she clamped her lips shut again, her shoulders falling. "I can't let you do that. It's too much."

He wasn't above playing the guilt card to get her to agree. After all, he was an expert at self-imposed guilt trips. Ultimately what he needed was time to convince Lauren not to marry Kelsey and this was his plan A, B and C. He had no other options.

"Tony often spoke to me about giving you a beautiful wedding when the time came. And, yes, I may have some reservations about how quickly this is all happening, but in my heart I know your brother would've wanted it this way."

Tears sprang to her eyes and she trembled. "Oh, Cooper."

And then she was in his arms, her supple, firm body plastered against him, her gratitude brimming. When she turned her head slightly, his nose was in her hair, her subtle, fresh, flowery scent teasing him.

"I take that as a yes," he whispered.

Her head bobbed up and down. "Yes," she said, raw emotion in her voice.

He glanced over at Loretta hopelessly.

A full-out approving smile graced her face and she gave him a big nod.

Which sort of worried him a bit, he wasn't gonna lie.

"I have the best news, Roger," Lauren said, coming to sit next to him on the den sofa in his penthouse apartment overlooking the Dallas skyline. The view here was amazing, just as amazing as the tall, dark-haired man she was to marry. She admired Roger's always-groomed look, his sense of style and his abundant confidence. Up until Tony died, she'd only seen Roger as a casual friend. But he'd been magnificent to her ever since the funeral and they'd had a whirlwind love affair. "My brother's best friend has offered us the use of his ranch to hold our wedding. Stone Ridge is magnificent. There's no need to have a simple courthouse wedding, after all. And Mama is pretty sure we can get it all together in a month."

Roger pursed his lips, deep in thought. "A ranch wedding?"

"Not just any ranch, honey. It's Tony's best friend Cooper Stone's ranch. You may have met him at the funeral." She hated bringing up that sad day. The memory still seared a hole in her heart.

"Sounds like a lot of work," Roger said. "Can't we just get married without all the fuss?"

Lauren shrugged, feeling deflated. "Yes, I suppose. But finally Mama is on board and even seems excited about planning the wedding with me. And, well, I've always dreamed about having a beautiful wedding."

Roger stared at her and then leaned forward and kissed her cheek. "Can we keep it small, at least?"

"Yes, of course. No more than one hundred people. I promise."

"A hundred?" His voice hit a high note. "That many?"

"That's not very many when we consider your employees and our mutual friends, plus my dear friends at the hospital. I'm so excited about this. Please, please, say it's okay with you."

He scratched his head. Roger didn't like to mingle and didn't like crowds. But a woman only got married once and she was sure he'd come around and be just as happy about the wedding plans as she was.

"Yeah, it's okay with me."

She bounded out of her seat, wrapped her arms around his neck and hugged him for all she was worth. "Thanks, Roger. You've made me very happy!"

"That's the plan, isn't it? Happy wife, happy life."

"Oh, we'll sure have that," she said, smiling. "I'm taking a good chunk of the vacation I've stored up to plan the wedding. Oh, Roger, it's gonna be so much fun."

"If you say so. But remember, I've got that big, new deal coming up this month. I'm going to be extremely busy."

"But not too busy to help with the wedding plans. I've always wanted a June wedding. I can't wait to start planning."

She got up from the sofa and grabbed her purse. "I'm off now. Mama and I have a date to start the plans."

Roger stood and walked her to the door. "Just don't break the bank on this," he said.

"Never. If I'm one thing, it's frugal. Had to be, with my dad leaving us and my mama a nurse. We didn't have much, but we always managed." With Tony's financial help, she'd made it through nursing school without having to take out a huge college loan.

Roger kissed her briefly. As she waved goodbye to him from the elevator, she took one last look at his apartment. With its sleek furniture and state-of-the-art kitchen, everything about the place screamed edgy. It was sure a far cry from the humble home she lived in with her mother on Masefield Avenue.

After Tony died, Lauren had given up an apartment she'd shared with a fellow nurse. Her mama needed her, but in truth, Lauren had probably gotten just as much comfort as her mother had from staying in her childhood home on the outskirts of town.

Pretty soon, though, once she married, she'd be living in the heart of Dallas with Roger.

The drive home at this time of evening wasn't easy. Dallas traffic bottled up and she found herself on the road rocking out to Carrie Underwood singing about bad boys and payback.

It was a good twenty minutes later when she pulled onto Masefield Avenue. A man holding a ledger under his arm was just leaving the house. He nodded to her.

"Evening, miss," he said.

"Hello." Puzzled, she slowed her steps and watched him get into a car and drive off.

She entered the house. "Mama?"

"In the kitchen, honey," Loretta said.

Her mama glanced at her as she stepped into the room. The table was littered with papers and paint samples. "Well, I finally got that estimate to paint the entire house, inside and out. And looks like if I agree to have them start tomorrow and pay them cash, he's gonna give me a nice discount."

"Mama? What are you talking about? We have a wedding to plan. We can't have painters in here."

"Honey, actually it's the perfect time to have the house painted. I've delayed it for so long because it's a nuisance to have workmen here and everything all covered up. You know what the smell of paint does to my sinuses. But, if we take Cooper up on his offer, we can move into his place until the wedding. That'll give the workmen more than enough time to get the house done."

"Mama, it was awfully sweet of Cooper to invite us to stay at his ranch, but he wasn't serious."

"Oh, yes, he was. He called up today asking when we were coming."

"He did not."

"He did. That Cooper is as fine as they come."

"He's still feeling guilty about Tony, Mama. That's all it is. He doesn't really want us underfoot."

"Well, it's too late for that now. I told him yes."

"Mama, you didn't." It wasn't like her mother to be this impetuous.

"Honey, this house hasn't been painted since your father left. You know how many years that's been? More than fifteen. The paint's peeling in every room!

I've got the money saved up for this, and it's the perfect time."

"But how...what am I supposed to... Mama, I can't believe you did this without checking with me first."

"It'll be fine, darling. You're taking time off to plan the wedding starting Monday so you won't have to commute to the hospital. It'll be like a little staycation, isn't that what they call it?"

"Yes, that's what it's called, but that means staying at your own house."

"Oh. Well, no matter. I've given Turner Painting a cash deposit. So pack a bag or two, sweetheart, and don't forget your wedding binder. We're moving to Stone Ridge tomorrow."

Two

On the drive out to Stone Ridge, Lauren couldn't stop wondering if she'd been bamboozled into moving into Cooper's house by her wily mother. Boy, when her mama put her mind to something, she was like a wrecking ball. That was one of the traits she loved most about her. And her mama wasn't about to let an opportunity like this one slip between her fingers. She wanted her house painted inside and out, and they didn't have the funds to move into a motel for the weeks it would take to finish the project. So what if her mother saw living at Stone Ridge as a perfect solution to a problem? Even Lauren saw the merits. It was just that…she didn't want to take advantage of Cooper.

Sure, he was wealthy and could afford having guests

in his home, especially if those guests were like family. Maybe he was lonely and wanted company.

She scoffed out loud at the thought.

"You say something, honey?"

She cleared her throat. "No, Mama. Just a little froggy."

Her mother smiled.

Cooper couldn't be lonely…not for female companionship, anyway. That man was hot with a capital H. Lauren had noticed. Any red-blooded woman would. And she wasn't going to beat herself up about how hard her heart pounded when he walked into a room. She'd crushed on him as a girl, and you never really get over first crushes. Especially if the crush had deep, sea-blue eyes, a square jawline and long, thick, dark blond hair. Especially if the man filled out his shirt with broad shoulders and granite arms.

Cooper Stone was all man, all Texan, all the time. She giggled.

"What's funny?" her mother asked.

"Nothing. Oh, look, Mama." She distracted her mama by pointing to the gates of Stone Ridge. "Gosh, I haven't been here in ages. I've forgotten how beautiful it is."

Acres upon acres of rich green pastures surrounded the property. This time of year, the dogwood trees that lined the road to the house were in full bloom, flourishing in pinks and whites. She recalled Cooper telling her years ago those trees were his mother's favorite thing about the ranch.

For Lauren, catching her first glimpse of the house

as they drove up was the ultimate experience. The design had a modern-day, country-home feel, with slate stone and cedar wood and a beautiful wood-framed, glass double-door entry. It was hardly a traditional ranch house from the past, but more a contemporary marvel.

The barns and stables were quite a distance off, so the scent of fresh blooms didn't have to battle with cattle smells and packed earth. It was something, this ranch, and suddenly inspiration hit, giving Lauren a million ideas for her wedding. She particularly noted the well-groomed garden leading up to the steps to the mosaic stone-front entrance.

She parked her Honda and took a breath. "Ready for this?"

Her mother only smiled. "You have no idea how much."

It did her heart good to see her mother finally coming around, finally warming to the idea of her marrying Roger. Once the initial shock had worn off, her mother seemed to be all-in.

Lauren was jumping over one hurdle at a time, heading toward the finish line.

It was awesome to feel this way. To know her life had direction. The shock of Tony's death had stymied her and she hadn't known where to turn. Then she'd starting dating Roger, and found him compassionate. They'd shared their grief over losing such a wonderful man and things just sort of rolled along from there. Up until that point, she hadn't had much luck in love.

Her friends said she was a dreamer, a passionate

soul who got restless too easily with the opposite sex. As grounded as she was in nursing, her private life hadn't been all too…stable.

Cooper drove up in his four-wheel-drive Jeep and pulled in front of her car, grabbing her attention. He parked, then gripped the roll bar in one hand and hopped out.

"Oh, look, there's Cooper," her mother said.

How could she miss him? He was slapping dust off his chaps and blue chambray shirt as he began his approach, his stride confident, his smile welcoming. All golden tanned and muscled, he sauntered over.

"Hey," he said.

The rich, deep tone of his voice made her gulp air. She'd grown up in Texas and rugged cowboys were a dime a dozen.

But Cooper Stone was in a class by himself. And the feminist in her said she could react this way about a handsome guy without tripping over guilt about Roger. Her fiancé.

Plus, Coop was doing her a big favor.

"Hi, Cooper. We made it," she said lamely. Of course, they'd made it. It wasn't as if she'd traveled across state lines to get there. Stone Ridge was a mere twenty miles from the Dallas city limits.

"I can see that." He ducked his head into the turned-down window, which brought his face within inches of hers. "Morning, Loretta."

"Cooper, it's good to see you. Looks like you're working already."

"I like to get my hands dirty every so often, reminds

me of my heritage." He winked. "I was helping my crew tear down an old shack we had on the property. Glad I made it back in time to greet you."

He pulled off his tan leather gloves and stuffed them into his back pocket. "Let me help you carry your luggage into the house," he said. "I'll show you to your rooms."

"Are you sure we're not putting you and Jared out? We don't want to get in your way," Lauren said. She'd never even considered the fact that this might inconvenience his brother, too.

"You're not putting me out," Cooper said automatically, which made her feel a ton better. "And my brother has his own place. He lives up the road at the other end of the pasture, and he's on board with having the wedding here."

"Good to know," she said. She didn't know Jared very well. He was younger than Cooper and Tony by a few years. She was happy that Jared didn't mind. "But if we ever get in your way, you just say the word and we'll make other arrangements."

"Lauren."

Okay, so maybe she was overdoing it, but Lauren wasn't too good at accepting big favors like this. Or was it something else, something that had to do with her breath catching as soon as Cooper smiled at her?

"We appreciate your hospitality, Cooper," her mother said.

"Anything I can do to help." He walked around the car and gave her mother a hand as she got out of her seat.

Lauren climbed out, as well, and popped her trunk. Her life for the next month was crammed into her luggage, four bags in all. Her mom had brought two bags.

Cooper walked to the trunk. He didn't blink an eye as he hoisted four of the bags like they weighed nothing. "I'll get the rest on my next trip out."

"I can get them," Lauren said, pulling two pieces of rolling luggage out and setting them on their wheels.

"Cooper, for heaven's sake, I'm not ancient," her mother said. "Give me one of those bags."

Copper grinned. "Sure thing." He handed her the smallest one. "Here you go."

In that one move, he'd saved her mother's pride, telling Lauren he had enough confidence in his own manhood to allow her mom to help. Lauren made a mental note. Add that to the growing list of things she found appealing about Cooper Stone.

Once inside, Cooper stood in the foyer and pointed to a wide, winding staircase. "I've given you both the rooms facing west. You'll see some amazing sunsets."

"Thanks, Cooper," she said. "Gosh, it's been so many years since I've been to your ranch. This place is completely transformed."

The living room was huge, with a floor-to-ceiling fireplace made with sleek slate and light wood. A sitting area faced the fireplace and another faced a set of windows overlooking the gardens and green pastures beyond. Overhead, thick beams lent a slightly rustic tone to the contemporary décor.

"I'll show you around a little later, after you get settled in." He began climbing the stairs and the two of them followed until they reached the first guest room.

"Oh, this is lovely," her mother said immediately.

"Then I chose correctly," he said. "I figured you'd like this room, Loretta."

It was bright and cheerful with white-shuttered windows and ivory furniture upholstered in a floral motif. The room almost looked too girly for a bachelor's ranch home.

Cooper dropped off her mother's bags and then led Lauren to the next guest room, done in light blues with pale gray walls and stained mango wood furniture that instantly made her feel at peace. "This is nice."

"Glad you like it." He set her luggage down on the bed. "Here you go. I'll see you later after a quick shower and change of clothes."

Her eyes dipped to his body, an involuntary movement that brought a flush to her cheeks. If he noticed, he didn't react.

"Okay, thanks again. See ya."

"Lauren," he said, a serious tone in his voice.

"What?"

"Stop thanking me. Please."

She scrunched up her face. She couldn't help it if her mother had drilled manners into her, could she?

"I'll try."

He gave her a nod. "Good enough."

And then he was out the door, heading for a shower.

This time, she forced an image of Roger into her head.

Yes, that was a nice, safe place to be.

* * *

Cooper pulled out a pitcher of lemonade just as Loretta walked into the kitchen. "My goodness, what a pretty kitchen you have."

Cooper only smiled. He'd had this house built seven years ago on the same spot as the old ranch house. His mother hadn't minded tearing the old place down. She was quite progressive and didn't like to dwell in the past. She and his dad had had a good life, but after he'd died, she'd spent all her energy on helping Cooper plan out a new modern-day version of the house. And his mother was a perfectionist, down to the last detail.

The enormous room had white cupboards, dark granite countertops and stainless-steel appliances. There was everything imaginable, from a brick oven to a six-burner stovetop with a covered grill to a table that seated eight. "My mom's doing."

"How is Veronica these days?"

"Mom's good. She's remarried, as you know, living down in Houston. Her husband keeps her pretty busy traveling."

"Well, you tell her I said hello next time you talk to her."

"Will do. Lemonade?"

"Sure, thanks."

He poured them both a glass and handed one to Loretta. "I'm glad you're here."

"Me, too," she said as she glanced out the kitchen doorway. "Cooper, I had to do some scheming to get my daughter here," she whispered. "But I know it's the right move. Otherwise, I'd never be so underhanded."

"What did you do?"

She smiled. "Hired a crew to paint my house inside and out."

He grinned. "Did you now?"

"Had to, and even paid them extra to get the crew to start today. I needed a reason to get Lauren to move out of the house. She's a little uncomfortable about it."

He knew the feeling. Hell, he hadn't had a woman here since he'd given up dating six months ago. Now he had two females under his roof. "She'll be fine. I'll try to ease her mind a bit."

Loretta's eyes softened. "You're a blessing, Cooper."

"I'm nothing of the sort, Loretta."

"You've got a good heart for doing this."

He scratched his chin. "About that, Loretta. I hope you know you're both welcome here, but I'm not exactly sure how this is all going to work. I mean, Lauren's set on marrying this guy and I can only do so much. I came up with this plan pretty quick and all." He hadn't really thought it through, but Loretta seemed set on breaking up Lauren's engagement, or at the very least, making sure Kelsey was an upstanding man, deserving of her daughter's hand.

The only real plan in his head was to keep watch over Lauren while he tried to find out Kelsey's true intentions. His gut was telling him her fiancé was no good, and he trusted his gut. If the guy had been cheating Tony, then he should be exposed for the creep that he was. Protecting Lauren was Cooper's job now…at all costs. If his secret plan went awry, he could lose Lauren's friendship, but it was a risk he was willing to take. He owed Tony that much. Hell, he owed the entire Abbott family.

Period.

"It's a start. We can keep an eye on Lauren better at your ranch, without too much interference from Roger," Loretta said, breaking into his thoughts. "We'll figure it out as we go."

That was an understatement.

"How's your brother?"

"Jared's good."

"Will we be seeing him while we're here?"

"From time to time. He's got an office up at his house and we have dinner a few times a week."

"You two boys have certainly made a success of this ranch," she said.

"We just picked up where Dad left off. He started the place and taught us the business. Luckily, we both love ranching. Jared's the brains and I'm the brawn in the duo." Cooper smiled and sipped lemonade.

Lauren walked in, her eyes taking in the entire kitchen. "Wow. A girl could go into crazy cooking mode in this place."

"Feel free. I'm sure Marie wouldn't mind a bit."

"Marie? Is she…?"

"She is. She's the same housekeeper we've had since I was a boy," he said, handing Lauren a glass of lemonade. "She's getting on in age, so we keep her duties light. She splits her time between here and Jared's place, but we've also got a cleaning crew that comes in to help her out," he explained. "Have a seat, ladies."

While they took their seats at the table, he scrounged

around for the oatmeal chocolate-chip cookies Marie had made yesterday. "Ah, here they are." He set the plate on the table. "Snacks. Have some."

"They look delicious," Loretta said, taking one.

"They are," Cooper said, gesturing for Lauren to take one, as well.

"If I do, then I'll have to jog another mile or two to work it off."

"You jog?"

She nodded. "Yes."

"And she does yoga, too," Loretta added.

"Well, I know nothing about yoga, but anytime you want a jogging partner, I'm your guy."

"Really?"

She seemed surprised and that surprised him. "Yep. What, you didn't think cowboys jogged?"

Lauren laughed. "Well, no. I guess I can't picture it."

"See me in the morning and I'll paint you that picture."

"You're on," Lauren said. She delicately picked up a cookie and took a small bite. "Oh, these are delicious." She began nodding her head. "I can see I'm going to need to step up my game if this is how Marie cooks."

"It is a challenge," Cooper admitted. "So, where would you like to start? I can show you around the house and then we can take a tour of the grounds. Were you thinking of a church wedding or having it here?"

"I'm…not sure. I'll have to speak to Roger about that. Up until a few days ago, we were going to the courthouse to get married."

Loretta frowned slightly. The idea of her daughter marrying this guy unsettled her, but she was hiding it well.

"I'm sure you have to get to work, Cooper," Lauren said.

"I have a few hours. Let me give you a tour of the house first."

After cookies and lemonade in the grand kitchen, Cooper began showing them the finer points of the room including how to work all the digital electronic appliances and how to turn on the television set in the refrigerator door, which also told the time and local temperature. By the time he was through, Lauren's head was spinning. But her mama took it all in stride as if she was tickled pink to be here.

Lauren still felt awkward about the entire situation.

"The kitchen is always available to you," he said. "If Marie's here, she's usually really good about having meals ready. If there's something you want, just ask her, and if she's not here, have at it. Feel free to cook something yourself."

"I think Lauren might take you up on that, Cooper," her mama said.

"Fine with me." Cooper's gaze connected with Lauren's and all that blue coming her way made her dizzy.

It was a mother thing, putting words in Lauren's mouth. She didn't like it, but her best friend Katy said her mother did the same thing to her quite a bit. And she had made that crack about *crazy cooking mode* earlier. Still, she wasn't at ease here yet. She hoped that would change.

Next, they followed Cooper through the living room and formal dining area, as well as a great room that housed a bar, a reading nook and a giant flat-screen television. The room was the coziest in the house, done in warm colors, with lived-in leather sofas and a rustic red-brick fireplace. He showed them how to turn on music from an in-wall stereo system with enough lights and buttons to rival an airplane dashboard.

Warning to self. Do not even think about it. She'd be sure to foul up the music system.

Then Cooper led them down the hall to his study, which he used as an office. Across the hall was a full state-of-the-art gym. "Wow," she said under her breath. Of all the things he'd showed her thus far, this was the only thing she really envied. "I'm impressed. Do you…?"

"Yep, I get my cowboy ass—uh, excuse me, Loretta—in here a few times a week."

"That's obvious," Lauren said without thinking. She resisted slapping her hand over her mouth. Goodness, she had to keep her lips buttoned more around him or he'd think she was flirting or something.

Cooper blinked once and then let the comment pass.

The gym had a shower area with a complete set of sundries, a sauna and an indoor Jacuzzi. Everything was framed in travertine and marble. The shower alone was bigger than a walk-in closet.

"Again," he said, "feel free to use anything here you'd like."

A sliding-glass door in the gym led them outside to the back of the house. The gardens were colorful, day lilies, peonies and primrose erupting into full bloom everywhere. A snow-white lattice gazebo sat smack in the middle of the grounds and off to the side crystal-blue waters flowed down a rock waterfall into a pool. A long stone-and-glass fire pit was surrounded by lounge chairs. It was perfection.

"It's like a resort," Loretta said.

Cooper laughed. "I used to throw some great parties here."

"Tony told me. He loved those parties."

Cooper's face fell. "I know. God, I miss him."

Lauren saw his pain and reached for his hand. "We all do." He stared into her eyes a moment and nodded. Her mama took both of their hands and squeezed. And they stood there for a while, hands entwined.

After a time, her mama spoke up. "Tony wouldn't want us to be sad. He'd want us to celebrate his life."

It was hard for Mama to be the cheerleader in this, but she had a point. Tony would hate their grieving. He would want them to get on with their lives. "You're right, Mama."

Cooper sighed with what seemed to be remorse.

"Well," Lauren said, contemplating their surroundings, "this place will make for a beautiful wedding. There's plenty of room to speak vows by the pool. Maybe under the gazebo."

"But Cooper has some other spots to show you, honey," her mother said. "Don't you, Cooper? You know, those places you told me about out by the lake."

"Yeah, I sure do," he said, coming out of his slump. "I was planning on taking you there today. That's if you're up to it."

"I'd love to see the lake," Lauren said.

"Actually, you two go on." Loretta briefly closed her eyes. "I'm a bit tired. I'd like go up to my room and take a rest."

"We can wait for you, Mama. Do it another time," Lauren said.

"Nonsense, Lauren. You need to work this out as soon as possible and Cooper has the time today."

"That's right. I sure do."

"Can I help you up the stairs?" she asked her mother as they went back inside and sat down.

"Lauren, I said I was tired, honey, not decrepit."

Out of the corner of her eye she saw Cooper try to hide a smile by twisting his mouth in an unbecoming way. Which was saying something, because Cooper was pretty much handsome no matter what kind of face he made. Then he faked a cough to contain a laugh, but her mother didn't seem to notice.

"Of course you're not decrepit, Mama." A nurturer by nature, the last thing Loretta wanted was to be deemed incapable of taking care of herself. Lauren should've known not to put it that way, but being here was a bit daunting, no matter how welcoming Cooper was at the moment. With planning her quickie wedding and all the changes in her life lately, Lauren was a little bit at loose ends.

She turned to Cooper, the tilt of her head telling him

she knew he'd been laughing at her. "Am I good to go like this?" she asked, gesturing to her attire.

"Let's see. Boots, jeans, check. The hat I'll take care of. Spring weather can be iffy. Do you want to bring along a light sweater?"

"Nah, I'll rough it. Besides, the sun is out and it doesn't look like it's going anywhere today."

"Okay, then I'll see you two later." Mama popped out of her chair like a piece of well-done bread from a toaster. "I'll just go up to my room now."

"Have a good rest, Loretta," Cooper said.

After her mother walked out of the room, Cooper turned to Lauren, a smirk emerging on his face again. She rolled her eyes.

"What?" he said, innocent as a baby.

"You're a brat, you know that, Cooper Stone."

"At least you aren't inferring I was decrepit."

She punched him in the arm. It felt good, to give back his teasing in a playful way.

"Ow." He put his hand over the arm she'd just whacked.

No way had she hurt him. Those muscles were like granite. A silly smile appeared on his face. "Now that's the Lauren Abbott I remember."

She smiled back. "Be careful or you just might see more of her than you want."

"That could only be a good thing," he said softly, placing his hand on the small of her back, grabbing his hat and leading her out the door.

The kind words and special touch brought familiarity.

And a mass of tingles she hadn't expected.

* * *

Cooper stood by the Jeep. "Drive or ride?" he asked Lauren.

Her pretty green eyes narrowed, as if she thought he was messing with her again. "Isn't it the same thing?"

"Well, I can drive us in the Jeep to see the grounds or we can mount up." He pointed to the stables just within eyeshot. "On a horse."

"Oh." She shook her head. "I haven't been riding in eons. I think the Jeep is the safest bet today."

"Okay. Another time," he said. He hadn't quite figured Lauren out. At times she seemed impetuous, a girl who liked to take a risk. That was the girl who'd punched him in the arm just a few minutes ago. That punch had surprised him in a good way.

She was back to being the girl he remembered, never taking any guff from anyone. Whenever Tony had teased her, she'd always shot back at him, giving as good as she got. Marrying Kelsey on a whim after six months of dating was another impulsive move on her part. That's why he was puzzled. Lauren seemed hesitant in coming here. Was she uncomfortable around him? Was she feeling manipulated into living at Stone Ridge for the month? Or was she having second doubts about the sudden marriage?

He hoped it was the latter. He hoped she'd put a halt to the wedding on her own terms so he could end this ruse. But at least having her here lent him the time he needed to find out what Kelsey was really up to. He could keep an eye on Lauren, as well.

"Hop in," he said, opening the door for her. She

climbed in and buckled her seat belt as he took his place behind the wheel. "Ready?"

"Ready."

He grabbed a tan suede hat from the backseat and plopped it on her head. It sank onto her forehead and pushed her blond locks down past her shoulders, making her look damn cute.

"This yours?" she asked.

"Uh-huh," he said. "Hang on to it when we take off."

Then he revved the engine and pulled away from the house.

After a minute she asked. "Where is the lake?"

"Back there." He gestured behind him. "We passed it a ways back."

"But aren't we going there?"

"Yep, but there's someplace else I thought you'd like to see."

"You're full of surprises, Coop."

He liked the sound of his nickname falling off her lips. That and the way she looked in his hat was messing with his head a little. "Not really. Pretty much what you see is what you get with me."

At least it always had been. Now he wasn't quite so sure. He'd surprised himself when he'd invited Lauren to have her wedding here. And he'd surprised himself even more by asking her to move into his house. He had underlying motives for having her here, true, and saving her from heartache would be something Tony would've wanted from him.

That one fact made all of this seem more palatable.

"Here we are," he said, stopping the Jeep in front of

a stand of shade-bearing oak trees. "We have to walk from here."

He came around the end of the Jeep and helped Lauren gain her footing as she got out. He held her steady and she gazed at him, gratitude glowing in her eyes. "I know where you're taking me."

His brows lifted. "You do?"

"Of course. Tony would talk about this place incessantly and I would be green with envy."

"Yeah, this was a special place to us," he said, taking hold of her hand. "Be careful, the land's uneven here. Lots of roots breaking through the soil."

They walked a bit, her hand gripped in his, reminding him just how long it'd been since he'd held a soft woman. And Lauren was that and more. He didn't like noticing her that way, or feeling even remotely attracted to her. She was cute and funny and nice. Emphasis on *nice.* Any other thoughts about her weren't going to happen. He had a job to do. Protect Lauren. Stop her wedding if need be. Make sure she didn't get hurt and pray she didn't hate him for the rest of her life.

"Just a little bit longer now."

And then he came upon his childhood fort, a mismatched set of planks built between the lower branches of a thick oak. The place looked the same as he remembered, though a bit more weathered, but the roof was intact and the wood beams were holding strong. A rope ladder, made of thick hemp, scraped against the dark tree bark.

"You're smiling so wide right now," Lauren said.

"Am I?" This place always made him happy.

"There's a twinkle in your eyes, too."

"Careful, Laurie Loo. I've never taken a girl here before. Don't make me regret it."

"Never. I'm glad to be here. I guess this is where you and Tony conspired."

"It is. Mostly we pretended to be looting pirates or badass cowboys. My dad gave us the wood and told us to have at it. I think we were ten at the time."

"So you built this all by yourselves?"

"Hell, no. After three attempts, my dad intervened. He said he didn't want us breaking our necks when the whole thing collapsed. But he taught us one important lesson."

"What was that?"

"That things aren't always as simple and easy as they initially seem. Your brother and I were so damn eager to do this on our own, certain we could figure it out. But after failing a few times pretty darn badly, we finally realized the project was too big for us. Our pride was bruised and we were embarrassed to ask for help after insisting we could do it all on our own. And Dad was great about it, without rubbing our noses in I-told-you-sos. He was proud of us for not giving up and for finding a way to make it happen."

"Wow. Your dad was pretty wonderful."

"He was a good man."

A sudden chilly breeze blew by and Cooper gazed upward. Clouds were moving in fast, turning the sky gray, and he caught Lauren trembling. "We should go. The weather's about to change and it can put you in a world of goose bumps. If we're lucky, we can make it to the lake before the wind gets out of hand."

"Sounds good," she said. "And thanks for bringing me here, Cooper."

"Welcome." He took her hand again. As they began to forge their way back to the Jeep, the air grew chillier, the clouds completely obscuring any sunlight.

"Damn," he said. "I think we're in for it."

"In for what?"

Suddenly, off in the distance, lightning ignited the sky. Clouds crashed against each other and rain poured down as if a giant water balloon had burst. Caught in a flash storm, they were getting soaked.

"Wow! That came on fast," Lauren said.

"Sure did." He gauged his options. "C'mon, let's make a run for it."

"Where?"

But he had already changed their direction. The Jeep would provide no protection. There was only one place to go. Still holding her hand, he guided Lauren along the muddied path leading them back to the fort.

Once they arrived, Lauren took a look at the ladder rope. "You're kidding, right?"

He shrugged. "Either that or get soaked to the bone." Which she already was. "C'mon. I'll help you up."

"Okay," she said tentatively.

And then she was climbing the rungs as he held the ladder firm, her butt in his line of vision. It was a beautiful sight, one he shouldn't be noticing. But he had to keep his eyes sharp, just in case she lost her footing. At least, that's what he told himself as she ascended the ladder.

She threw herself inside the fort and he followed her. They nestled together against the back wall, out of the spray of raindrops. Lauren shivered, her blouse soaked and plastered to the beautiful swells of her breasts. The transparency was hard to miss and, for a moment, Coop couldn't tear his gaze away. Then sanity rushed in. He began unbuttoning his shirt. "Here you go. Put this on."

Her face flushed cherry-red. She was aware of the sight she made. She accepted his shirt without argument and he helped her put her arms into the sleeves. "Thanks."

She hugged her knees to her chest and sighed. "Well, guess I was wrong."

"About?" He sat next to her, in his undershirt, his legs straight out, his boots just inside the confines of the fort.

"The weather."

It was too much to hope she'd admit she was wrong about marrying Kelsey. Wishful thinking never got him anywhere. He'd have to tell Loretta his suspicions and start scouring Tony's computer for hints that Kelsey had been cheating the business. And he'd have to start as soon as possible.

"It's actually pretty cool to be here, storm and all," she said. "Tell me more about you and Tony. What did you do when you came here?"

"I already told you," he said. "Pirates and cowboys."

She nodded, seeming suddenly sentimental. "Isn't there more?"

"We'd bring our lunches and eat, and then sometimes just lie back, sort of like we're doing now, and dream."

"What did you dream about?"

"Growing up. Racing cars. Dating girls. Boy stuff. I remember one of the last times we ever came here. I think we were fifteen. Samantha Purdue had broken up with Tony. He was crushed. We came up here with a six-pack of beer I'd swiped from home and chugged while he cried his eyes out."

"Wow. Over Samantha Purdue?"

"Yeah, it was stupid. The very next week, Tony was crushing on another girl." The memory made Cooper smile. "Your brother was girl-crazy."

"Maybe that's why he never married. What about you?"

"Me?" He shook his head. "I wasn't girl-crazy. More like, girls made me crazy."

She chuckled and a drop of rain fell from her hair and drizzled down her cheek. He braced her face in his hand and wiped away the rain with the pad of his thumb. Her skin was the softest silk. She smiled sweetly at him then, and something shifted in his chest.

"I meant why didn't you ever marry," she said quietly, gazing at him with those pale green eyes.

The impact of her question shook him to the core. He had no right touching her this way. He dropped his hand from her face and looked out at the driving rain. "I had some serious relationships in the past. They didn't work out. There's time for me."

"So you do want to marry eventually?"

"Yeah. One day. In the very, very distant future." Right now, women were off the table for him. He'd purged his "little black book." He was officially taking a break.

"And you? Did you ever imagine yourself getting married so young?"

"Young? I'm twenty-six. In the olden days, I'd be considered a spinster."

"Yeah, but it's not the olden days."

"I know, Coop. It's just that I've been kinda boy-crazy all my life. No one ever stuck. Maybe it runs in our DNA. Maybe Tony and I weren't very different from my father," she said quietly. "I've always worried about that. My father never seemed satisfied with what he had. You know his history, four marriages and divorces."

"Nah, you're not like him."

"I'd crush on one boy and then another, and I never wanted to settle."

"You shouldn't settle. Ever. You should be dead sure."

"My friends tease me about it, but Mama says it's just that my heart is big and it takes a whole lot to fill it."

"And Roger does that for you?"

Lauren bit her lip, hesitating for a fraction of a second too long. "Yeah, he does."

He wasn't convinced and, when she trembled, he wrapped his arm around her shoulders and pulled her in tight, warming them both up.

He hoped like hell Kelsey was true blue.

Otherwise he'd have to punch the guy's lights out and send him packing.

Three

After dinner that night Cooper sat facing Loretta in the dining room while Lauren was in the kitchen, cleaning up. "That was about the best darn chicken soup I've ever had," he said. "But don't tell Marie I said so."

"I won't," Loretta answered, beaming. Apparently after her rest, Lauren's mom had decided soup and homemade biscuits would be perfect on a rainy day. And she'd been right.

"Thanks for cooking tonight."

"Of course. It's my pleasure and the least I can do. What do you do when Marie isn't here to cook for you?"

"I scrounge around for leftovers. Marie's pretty good about making extra for the nights she's not here. Or I order in or scramble an egg or something."

"An egg? I can't imagine that would fill you up at all, Cooper."

"Well, I don't do that often. I've been known to meet up with a friend for dinner."

"A female friend?" Loretta asked coyly.

He grinned. "Don't have too many females in my life right now. Aside from you and Lauren."

"I think we're probably all you can handle right now. Don't you?"

He grinned. "Absolutely. Listen, while I have you alone, I need to tell you something. Come into the study with me. I don't want Lauren to overhear."

"Fine. I'll follow you."

He led Loretta down the hall and into his study and promptly closed the door. He didn't have much time, and he'd rehearsed how he was going to put this to cause her the least amount of grief.

"Loretta, I have a confession to make. Please sit down."

She stared at him curiously for a moment and then settled on the sofa. He took a seat on the opposite end.

"What is it?"

"It's just that when you approached me about Lauren and her decision to marry so quickly, it made me think of something Tony had told me just prior to the accident. I didn't want to bring it up at the time because it could be painful, but now that we're in this full speed, I need to tell you the truth."

"And that is?"

"Tony told me that he didn't trust Roger Kelsey. He thought his partner was cheating him and up to no good with the company. Tony was trying to get proof and confront him."

"You mean Roger was stealing from my son?"

"Yeah, that's what Tony seemed to think when he confided in me. Of course, he would've never approved of Lauren marrying the guy. It was the deciding factor in me helping to break up this wedding. Tony had good instincts and I trust that he was going to get that proof, but then the accident happened."

"Well, now…that makes it all the more important that Lauren break up with him."

"Yeah, that's how I see it."

"What if we told Lauren about Tony's suspicions?" Loretta asked. "Surely she'd take Tony's word over his."

"We have no proof. If we tell Lauren now about Tony's suspicions and she confronted Kelsey, it would give him time to cover his tracks and then we may never find out the truth. If the guy is that cagey, he'll win Lauren over and prove that he's straight as an arrow. Then she'll…"

"Blame us for interfering."

"Exactly. I'm sorry, Loretta."

She took his hand and squeezed. "No, I'm glad you told me. I only wish Tony would've shared this with me."

"I'm sure he didn't want to burden you and, of course, at the time, Lauren wasn't involved with Kelsey."

"That's true. And I was always saying that I didn't know a thing about real estate." Tears dripped from her eyes. "I never showed much interest in my Tony's business."

"He loved you, Loretta. And was so proud of you. He'd tell everyone you were the best nurse in the Lone Star State."

"Thanks, Cooper. I appreciate that, and I know that's how Tony felt. He would tell me that often." She straightened in her seat, no longer sorrowful. Instead a protective glint filled her eyes. "Now this sudden engagement makes all the more sense to me."

"Yeah."

"My Lauren is going to get hurt."

"I hope not. I'll do my best to make sure of it."

"Thank you, Cooper."

"So, that said, I'm going to need to get into Tony's laptop. Do you have it?"

She thought a moment. "Yes. I think I do. Most of his personal things are in boxes in my garage."

"Great. I'll need to get into that, if it's okay with you."

"Of course, it's okay. I'll make some excuse to go home tomorrow and get it for you. Cooper, should we alert the authorities about any of this?"

"Not now. We have nothing but Tony's suspicions. And on the slim chance that this guy wasn't cheating Tony, Lauren would probably never forgive either of us for going behind her back and causing her fiancé grief."

"Good point," she said with a nod, although her shoulders slumped in defeat.

Yeah, this was going to cause the Abbotts pain.

No matter what Cooper found.

* * *

Lauren had been jogging ever since college, but keeping pace with Cooper this morning was proving harder than she thought. He took it seriously and, given that he was six-foot-two, his strides were much longer than hers. Ten minutes into the run, she broke out into a sweat trying to keep up. After another ten minutes she was lagging, but as soon as he noticed, he slowed his pace. "You want to head back?" he asked.

"Not on your life," she answered. "And don't slow down for me. You can go on ahead."

He wasn't hard to watch from behind. He wore a Rangers baseball cap flipped backward on his head, a black tank exposing thick, tanned, muscular arms and a pair of gray sweatpants. Stripped down like this, the cowboy could pass for a city dude.

"Nah, I like the company."

"Don't ruin your workout for me."

"You're only making it better, Laurie Loo."

She laughed at his attempt at charm, but did appreciate him slowing down a bit. At this point, he'd taken her past his stables and corrals and then down a service road. The dawn air was cool but the sunshine overhead promised to dry out all the places the storm had muddied the day before.

She was able to take in more of the Stone Ridge scenery at this much slower pace than during yesterday's drive in the Jeep. They passed green pastures, lush from spring rain, with cattle grazing in groups. Every so often Cooper would lead her through a patch of shade from an oak or mesquite tree, providing temporary shelter from the dawn sunshine.

As they were rounding a bend, the lake came into view, a picturesque vision of tall trees reflecting off the waters lit by a stream of sunshine. Glossy and smooth as glass, the small lake was postcard ready and a perfect place to speak vows.

Lauren stopped running. "Oh, Coop."

He turned around, but kept running in place.

"This is amazing. What's it called?"

"The lake."

"The lake? You mean you don't have a name for it?"

"No. We've always just thought of it as the lake."

"Oh, man. That's a shame. Something this beautiful should have a name."

He shrugged. "C'mon. Let's see it closer up."

They jogged together until they reached the bank. Lauren sipped from her water bottle and gazed at the snow-white ducks flying in, taking a dip, splashing water everywhere and then taking off again. On the opposite bank, a mama duck waddled out of the water, her six little ducklings following behind, disappearing into the dark shade of an oak tree.

"I can picture my wedding here," Lauren said. A sense of wonder and awe filled her inside. She could see it all in her mind: chairs decorated with big bows set out in rows on the thick grass, a canopy of woodsy flowers over the archway where they would speak their vows. This was more her style, making a commitment outdoors, the natural surroundings seeming to convey a sense of truth and honesty. "I think this is the place."

She turned to Cooper, expecting to see him nod in agreement, or at least smile, but he was deep in thought. Heavy thought, it appeared, as his mouth was pulled down into a frown. Was he thinking about Tony?

"Coop?"

"Yep," he said, masking whatever emotion he was feeling by plastering on a smile. "I heard you. This is the place."

"Yes, thanks for bringing me here. I can't think of a better spot to be married."

"Okay, then," he said sharply. "Settled."

"Yeah," she said. He was struggling hard to maintain a smile. "Unless, you'd rather we do it somewhere else. Maybe you'd like to save this place for when you get married?"

"Hell, no. That's not happening anytime soon, Lauren. I brought you here, remember? If you want a lakeside wedding, that's what you'll have."

Still, his tone left her wondering. "Are you thinking about my brother?"

"I won't lie. Tony's been on my mind a lot lately."

"If it's too much for you to walk me down the aisle, Coop, please let me know."

"It's not that, Lauren. I'm honored to walk you down the aisle. But something keeps niggling at me. I don't see what the rush is all about."

"That's because you don't get me."

"I don't?"

"No, and neither does Mama. I've been impetuous in the past so I understand your skepticism, but I'm sure this time. I know what I want."

"Okay, if you're sure."

But even as he said it, the words rang…not false, but off somehow.

"I'm sure. Thanks again, for everything you're doing."

"Happy to do it," he said and then took hold of her hand. "C'mon. Let's walk back to the house now."

"Okay, sure." She turned around to give the lake one last glimpse. "I can't wait to tell Roger. Would you mind terribly if he came out to see the lake sometime?"

"Don't mind at all."

"I'm so excited."

"I'm…glad."

A short time later she entered the house alone and dashed up the stairs, eager to share the news with her mama. Cooper had excused himself, stopping at the stables to speak with his foreman.

She knocked on the bedroom door. "Mama, it's me."

"Come in, honey."

Lauren walked into the room as her mother was combing her hair. She wore it up most the time in a stylish twist with stray chocolate brown tendrils streaming down. "I was just getting ready to head out."

"Where are you going?"

"I have to speak with the painting contractor today," she said, giving her hair one final glance in the mirror. "He had some questions and wanted my approval on some things."

"Would you like me to go with you?"

"No, it's not necessary, honey. I thought I'd stop by Sadie's while I'm there. She's not been feeling well."

"Sorry to hear about Sadie. What's wrong with her?"

"She's feeling very tired lately. And that's unlike her. Usually she can run circles around me. She seemed out of breath when we spoke on the phone. So, what's got your eyes twinkling this morning? I know when something makes my girl happy."

"I am happy. Actually, I'm thrilled. I found the place where Roger and I are going to say our vows. Cooper and I jogged over to the lake earlier. It's perfect, Mama. Just like a dream."

"A dream, huh? That's saying something."

"Yes, I can't wait for you to see it."

"I'm sure I will. In due time."

"Mama?"

Her mother grabbed her hands and squeezed. "I'm just as thrilled as you are, sweetheart. But I've got this appointment today and I'm a bit worried about Sadie, so I've got to run."

"Sure, Mama. I'll show you the lake another time. You'll think it's perfect, too."

Her mother kissed her on the cheek. "'Bye, sweetheart."

"See you later, Mama."

Her mother picked up her purse and dashed out the door.

Lauren blinked. Their conversation sure seemed strange, as if she'd caught her mother red-handed today. She seemed guilty about something. Out at the lake, she'd gotten a similar "off" vibe from Cooper. Was there something in the coffee this morning?

She shoved her misgivings aside. Now that she knew

exactly where the wedding was to be held, she could concentrate on the next order of business in planning her perfect day.

Later that morning, after a shower and making some phone calls, Cooper drove up the road to speak with Jared. They had contracts to discuss but, more importantly, he needed to explain what was going on with Lauren and Loretta. Four years younger in age, Jared had a sensible head on his shoulders. He was the money man in the family. While Cooper ran the everyday workings of Stone Ridge along with Jim Bartlett, his foreman, Jared made sure all the numbers added up. They were two halves of a whole when it came to the ranch.

Now, sitting in his brother's kitchen, Cooper explained about his part in stopping Lauren's wedding.

"Are you nuts?" His brother's forehead wrinkled in four parallel lines.

"I probably am," he said. "But what choice do I have? Loretta is concerned about Lauren. And so am I. If she's being used and taken advantage of, I can't allow it."

"*You* can't allow it?"

"Yes, bro. Tony would never want his little sis to marry this guy if he's only trying to get control of the entire company."

"And now that's your problem?"

"Yeah, I suppose it is. Loretta came to me for help and I couldn't refuse her. I just couldn't."

"Lauren knows nothing about this?"

"Not a thing. She thinks… I'm some sort of saint for offering to have her wedding at the ranch. And, bro, she asked me to walk her down the aisle." He gulped air, his gut churning at the notion.

Jared ran his hand down his face. "Man. Are you sure you know what you're doing?"

"No. But I have to help Loretta and try to keep Lauren from getting hurt. And there's something else. I'm swearing you to secrecy here."

"You can trust me."

"Hell, if I can't trust you…never mind. The deal is, Tony confided in me that he thought Kelsey was manipulating the numbers and cheating him. Tony didn't trust his partner and was in the process of investigating it on his own. And I thought, if I could find some proof, that would be enough to convince Lauren to break it off with him. If we go to her without proof, she probably wouldn't listen. She'd think it was her mother's way of interfering, since Loretta has already tried to convince Lauren it's too soon and she shouldn't rush into marriage. But the fact is, Kelsey only showed interest in her after Tony died."

"Sounds suspicious to me."

"Yeah, I know." Cooper sighed. "Loretta's getting Tony's laptop out of storage today and I'll scour the thing and see what I can find."

"If you need help with that…"

"I was hoping you'd say that. You're the numbers man in the family. I just might take you up on the offer."

"Sure, I'll help. But, Coop," he said, "tread lightly.

This could all blow up in your face. If Lauren gets wind of what you're doing, she'd never forgive you. And if you and Loretta are wrong, again, you stand to lose family friendships over this."

"I'm hoping it doesn't. All I can do is try."

"And in the meantime, you've got Loretta and Lauren living at the ranch for the next few weeks?"

"Yeah."

Jared's head tilted a bit. "I saw Lauren at the funeral. She's all grown up now. Very pretty."

He'd noticed. "Your point?"

Jared began shaking his head. "She's living under your roof."

"So is Loretta. Again, your point?"

"Just be careful, Coop. That's what I'm saying."

Careful? If he was careful, his best friend wouldn't be dead. If he was careful, two women wouldn't be living with him at the ranch. If he was careful, he wouldn't have concocted this crazy scheme. "I'm afraid it's too late for careful."

Jared's chuckle grated in his ears. "All right then, just be…smart."

Smart had nothing to do with it. What he needed was luck.

An hour later, Cooper drove away from Jared's home, slightly relieved his brother now knew the situation and had his back. He parked the Jeep in the garage and entered his house to the sound of giggles coming from the kitchen. Heading toward the laughter he found Marie serving Lauren and her friend Katy homemade ice cream. Chocolate mint with brownie chunks. The women were lapping up the cones and smiling like little girls.

"Hi, Cooper," Lauren said. "You remember my best friend, Katy Millhouse, right?"

Katy, a brunette with big brown eyes and an engaging smile, waved. "Hi, Cooper. It's nice to see you again."

"Same here, Katy. Welcome to Stone Ridge. How've you been?"

"I'm doing well. Marie just made my day. This ice cream is delish."

"Want one?" Marie asked him, her kind, light blue eyes twinkling. She held a cone in her hand and was scooping away.

His longtime housekeeper knew him so well. He had trouble resisting delicious things, but he really shouldn't stick around. He should let Katy and Lauren get on with their business. With the laptop on the table and papers strewed all over, it looked like they were heavy into wedding planning.

Crap. His gut clenched. She was really going to do this thing. And he was really going to try to stop her.

He couldn't very well refuse a cone already scooped and ready to go. "Sure thing. Thanks, Marie."

He took a seat at the table and she handed him his cone. "Here you go."

He plunged in, taking a big lick, and glanced at Lauren, who was doing the same. Her tongue darting out to circle the top of her cone, her eyes closing at the taste and the luscious throaty sounds coming from her mouth were more than mildly erotic. The cone nearly dropped from his hand. What the hell? He had to stop noticing things like that about Lauren.

He averted his gaze, making eye contact with Katy instead, and the ridiculous fast beats of his heart slowed to normal.

"Katy's going to be my maid of honor," Lauren said to him.

"A good choice. Congrats, Katy."

"I'm super excited, Cooper," Katy said. "We've been talking about weddings and marriage since junior high school and…well, everyone always thought I'd marry first, since Lauren is so—"

Lauren shot her a look.

"Picky," Katy said slowly, garnering a nod from her friend. Cooper wondered what she'd really meant to say. "But she finally found the right guy."

"Picky?" he asked.

"You know, she could never make up her mind. She always had crushes on guys and dated a lot in high school and then in college—"

"There was only one guy in college, Katy. Remember?" Lauren said a little defensively.

"Oh, right, right. But all that's changed now. She's marrying Roger. It's going to be perfect."

Cooper gave Katy a smile. What else could he do but keep quiet, finish his cone and get out of there, pronto. He took one last big bite of the ice cream. "Delicious as always, Marie. I'll be in my office if you need me." He rose from the table.

"Oh, um…" Lauren began. "We were wondering if you could help us out. I promise it won't take long, but we're stuck on two different invitations and Marie likes them both equally. We need another opinion."

Cooper glanced at Marie, standing at the sink, shrugging her shoulders. She was so darn diplomatic she wouldn't want to influence the decision. He was trapped. He'd promised he'd help Lauren with any of the planning, if she needed it.

"Okay, sure. I've got a few minutes."

Lauren gestured for him to take a seat next to her. He did so hesitantly, and Lauren scooted her chair closer, pulling the laptop in front of both of them. Katy sat next to him on the other side, but it was only Lauren's sweet strawberry scent that filled his nostrils, only Lauren's arm accidently brushing his, that brought him up short. It didn't help that his brain was revisiting the image of Lauren licking at her ice-cream cone just a few minutes ago.

"So, it's between these two," she said, pulling up the invitations on the screen. "We're limited in choices because of such short notice. This company promises to overnight them to us, so we can get the invitations out immediately."

"I've already sent out email Save the Dates," Katy offered.

This was all above his pay grade. What did he know about Save the Dates and wedding invitations?

But Lauren was asking his advice and he kept telling himself it was what she would've asked of Tony, if he were still here.

"What do you think?" she asked.

He gazed at the two images side-by-side on the

screen. One was bold, with modern lines and block print on pure white paper. The other had soft, flowing script on ivory paper. It wasn't hard for him to choose. "This one," he said, pointing to the latter. "It reminds me of you."

"It does? Why?" Lauren asked, blinking her eyes.

"Because it's sort of gentle and understated and easy."

"Easy?" She laughed. *Shoot...* That wasn't what he meant at all.

Beside him, Katy chuckled.

"I mean, it's not as chaotic as the first one. It's easy to read, everything seems to flow. Hell, I don't know, Lauren. What does Kel—uh, Roger say?"

"Roger's not into planning the wedding. He's very busy right now. He says, whatever I want. As long as I don't break the bank."

"He put her on a budget," Katy added.

Cooper turned to face her. "Did he now?"

"Considering, he thought we were going to get married by the justice of the peace or something," she said, her voice dropping to a whisper, "he's being very generous."

And was probably using the money he'd cheated Tony out of to finance the wedding. "Generous? I thought the groom was supposed to grant the bride's every wish," he said as kindly as possible.

Lauren glanced at him thoughtfully. "I suppose. But Roger's not into all this wedding stuff."

"Maybe he should be," Cooper said. "You deserve the wedding of your dreams."

Lauren's face fell, and he kicked himself for putting it so bluntly. But every doubt he could plant in her mind, helped his cause.

He could also point out that she now owned half of the real-estate development firm of Kelsey-Abbott. She could spend some of that cash on her wedding if she wanted to. But he didn't want her losing any money if the wedding didn't happen, so he kept that thought to himself.

Let Kelsey take the hit when the wedding didn't happen. It would serve the guy right.

As soon as Cooper left the room, Katy grabbed Lauren's attention. "Oh, my goodness. Cooper is such a hunk."

"A hunk?" Lauren tried her best to sound nonchalant. It wasn't as if she hadn't noticed. Cooper Stone wasn't a man a girl could ignore. He had rugged features, dark blond hair and mesmerizing eyes. Not to mention a solid muscled-packed body. But Cooper had always turned her head and he'd been one of her big crushes when she was younger. She'd just gotten used to the fact that he was deliciously manly. "I suppose he is."

"You suppose? Is he dating anyone?"

"Not that I know. But he doesn't exactly confide in me about his love life."

"If he did have a girlfriend, I'd imagine she wouldn't take too kindly to having you living here with him."

"For heaven's sake, Katy. Mama's living here, too, and…well, he's not that irresistible that I can't keep my hands off. He's like family. And you're forgetting that Roger is the man I'm marrying."

"I know all that." Katy got dreamy-eyed, her expression going mushy soft. "But a girl can fantasize, can't she?"

"*You* certainly can, but keep me out of those fantasies." Yet having Katy think of Cooper in those terms didn't set right. She didn't want Cooper to star in any woman's fantasies. How bizarre was that?

"You went jogging with him this morning. How does he look in his running gear?"

"Katy!"

Her friend grinned wickedly and then they both burst out laughing.

After their chuckling died down, Katy got serious. "Now that Cooper helped you pick out the invitations, we have to find you a dress. We can get something off the rack. They have some really good buys this time of year. And a fitting shouldn't—"

"I have a dress."

"You do?"

"Yes, I've decided to wear Mama's dress. She's kept it in pristine condition all these years and it'll be a nice touch."

"I've seen your mom and dad's wedding picture. It's a lovely dress but, honey, it's a little outdated, isn't it?"

"It is. But I'd pay a fortune in a bridal salon for a vintage dress like this one. I've discussed it with Mama and she's thrilled to have me wear her dress."

"Thrilled?"

"Well, as happy as she can be. She's still not totally

convinced I should get married after dating Roger less than six months."

"But you are sure, right?"

"Of…course. I'm sure," she said. "He's a good guy."

"And you love him?"

"Yes." She didn't hesitate. She only wished Roger would be more interested in their wedding. She needed his input, but he was a busy man and some guys just weren't into all the fuss involved with planning a wedding. At least, that's what she'd read in several bridal magazines. She shouldn't feel bad, but instead just look at it as an advantage. The bride got her choice on everything. She'd adopted that line of thinking, to keep from being disappointed.

"Okay, we're checking off boxes and accomplishing a lot. Next, we need to pick out the menu for the wedding dinner. You have an idea of what you want, right?"

"I sure do." Lauren opened her bridal journal and turned to the pages that dealt with food options. Through the years, she'd managed to collect pictures and recipes of only the most elaborate meals to serve at the wedding.

"This looks delicious," Katy said, pointing to a French dish that only a chef of the highest caliber could create.

"I bet it is." Lauren sighed.

She glanced through the rest of the meals, shaking her head as she flipped from one page to another. All the dishes she'd picked were way out of her league. While she'd had a blast choosing items to go inside the book, she hadn't been practical. Not at all.

"I can't use any of this," she said to Katy, slamming the book closed. "It's time for a reality check. Let's compile a list of local caterers and see what they have to offer."

"Sounds like you're thinking practically now. Okay, let me work on that. I'll make some calls and get a few referrals. You can work on the music."

"Music?"

"Yeah, you'll need a band to play at the reception, right?"

"A band? I hadn't thought of that. Can't I hire a DJ?"

"Well, sure. You could. But I'm thinking there's so many starving musicians in Dallas who would love to play at your wedding. And remember, Jodie's brother is in a country band. She told me he's playing in a roadhouse not too far from here. You could scope the band out with Roger and see if it works."

Jodie Canton was Katy's coworker at the *Dallas Post*, the local newspaper. They were both associate editors. "You think so?"

"Live music is really a nice touch and I bet you could get them for what you'd pay a DJ."

"Really? A live band could be fun. I'll run it by Roger and see what he thinks."

"Okay, great. Now onto the flowers…"

Two hours later after Katy left, Lauren speed-dialed Roger's number. He didn't pick up right away and then, after five rings, answered abruptly. "What?"

"Hi, honey. Did I catch you at a bad time?"

He sighed and his exasperation came through loud

and clear. "No. It's fine. I'm a little busy. What's up, Lauren?"

"Uh, well. I just wanted to go over some of the plans I'm making with Katy, to make sure I'm on the right track."

"Can we do it another time?"

"Sure…if you're too busy. But, Roger, you haven't seen the ranch yet. I really wish you could spare some time to see it." *And me.* She hadn't seen him in several days. "It's where we'll say our vows," she said, unable to hide her disappointment.

"Okay, sweetheart," he said, softening his tone, as if he'd read her mind. "I promise to come by tomorrow afternoon. You can tell me everything then, all right?"

"Yes. Oh, I can't wait to see you."

"Me, too," he said. "Love ya, Lauren."

"Love you, too."

She hung up the phone and the nagging teensy doubt in her head vanished. She did love Roger. And he loved her. They were going to have a wonderful life together.

"Mama's gonna be a little late tonight," Lauren said to Cooper as he walked into the kitchen. She was still sitting at the kitchen table in front of her computer, where he'd left her and Katy hours ago. "She said not to wait on dinner."

"Anything wrong?" Cooper leaned against the granite counter, admiring Lauren's shoulder-length hair, the sunshine pouring in and highlighting the blond strands.

"I hope not. She's visiting our neighbor Sadie tonight. Mama's got a big heart. And Sadie lives alone.

If she's not feeling well, my mother wouldn't leave her. She's got a nurturing nature."

"Probably why she became a nurse."

"You know, I couldn't imagine her doing anything else with her life," Lauren said.

"And what about you?"

"I love nursing, too. It feels sort of weird, you know. Taking this vacation and not being at the hospital. I've never taken a month-long break."

"You making progress with the wedding plans?"

"Yes. Katy's been a big help. Otherwise, I think I'd go crazy with all the details."

"Something tells me you can handle it, Lauren."

She gazed at him with those killer meadow-green eyes. "Thank you," she said softly.

He pushed away from the counter and opened the fridge. "So, are you getting hungry?"

"I could eat."

"That's good, because I'm starving. Let's see what Marie left for us."

Behind him, he heard Lauren closing down the laptop and rising from her chair. A flowery scent invaded his nostrils as she sidled up next to him.

"Looks like roasted chicken and potatoes. And there's salad, too."

"Let me take care of this," she said, bumping hips to move him away. The contact of her body surprised him. In a very good way that was all wrong. "It's the least I can do." He stood aside, watching her pull the pan out of the fridge, backing out butt-first, her blond locks falling onto her face.

She's Tony's sister. She's Tony's sister. Yet his heart pumped a little faster anyway and he didn't like where his mind was going.

"You've been inside all day. Wanna have our meal out on the patio?" He needed air. And a way to distance himself from her. As big as his house was, it seemed awfully small in the kitchen with Lauren bustling around like she belonged there.

"Right, slaving away at my computer is tough work," she joked. "But eating outside does sound pretty nice. Let me heat up the food and set the table."

"I'll help," he said to be mannerly. He took the pan of roasted chicken out of her hands and they worked like a team reheating the meal in the oven and getting dishes down from the cupboard.

"You're pretty handy to have around." She walked out the wide doors leading to the patio, holding plates, forks and knives. He followed behind with two stemmed glasses, a corkscrew and a bottle of wine.

She set out the dishes and utensils and turned, giving the bottle in his hand a glance before lifting her pretty eyes to him.

"Would you rather have soda or tea?" he asked. What was he thinking? Wine was a bad idea.

"I love wine."

"Pinot okay?"

"I love Pinot." She chuckled and shook her head.

"What?"

"Nothing really. It's just you don't strike me as the Pinot type."

"I don't? What do I strike you as?"

"Beer. And not that light kind, but ale. Yeah, I can picture you gulping from a tall mug of ale."

"Like a pirate or something?"

Lauren tilted her head and studied him.

His facial scruff was in need of a good trim and his hair was probably sticking out in all four directions. But it wasn't disapproval on her face, and her smile radiated toward him, warm and inviting. The green in her eyes deepened to sage as she thought about it.

"Yeah, like a pirate, Cooper."

He studied her. She was dressed casually in a pair of jeans and a blue tank, her skin looking creamy-smooth under the fading sunlight. "But the cowboy in me prefers whiskey, straight up."

"Do you now?"

He nodded, gazing into her smiling eyes. "Yep."

It felt too much like flirting, something he had mastered before he'd given up women. A shudder ran the length of him. He was in uncharted territory. Lauren was a friend. She was also someone else's fiancée. He had to remember that. "I'll…go get the food." And before she could protest, he ordered, "Have a seat, Lauren."

A few minutes later he returned and sat still as an oak as Lauren served him his meal. She'd insisted on dishing up the food. The sky was burnt orange now, the sun low on the horizon, and the air was just the right side of cool. Once he got Lauren talking about being a nurse, all he had to do was feed his face and listen. But even the listening wasn't easy. Her voice, so animated, so suddenly, sweetly passionate, touched him deep down. He finished his meal and leaned way back in his seat, sipping wine. Every so often he had to look away, pretending interest in the sunset, fighting a war going on inside his head.

"Coop?"

"Hmm." He turned to face her.

"Am I boring you? I've been rattling on."

He smiled. "I don't mind. Sorta nice hearing how much you enjoy your work."

Her brows rose in skepticism and she sipped the last of her wine. Her glass landed in a soft clink on the table. "That was delish."

"Want more?"

"No," she said, shaking her head. "I'm a lightweight. Two's more than enough. In fact, I'm feeling a bit buzzed. After I do the dishes, I think I'll take a walk to clear my head."

"You don't have to do dishes."

"In my head, I do. So, no arguing."

"Fine. The dishes will keep. Take your walk now while there's still some light."

"Okay, I will. But those dishes better be here when I get back."

"Yes, boss."

"It was really nice having dinner on the patio."

He gave her a look.

"I know, I know. I'm burning sunlight."

He laughed and waited until she was out the front door and down the path, to step onto the veranda. As long as Lauren was walking straight, which she was, he could put aside his doubts about letting her go alone. Her buzz couldn't be that bad, could it?

Once she was out of sight, he turned to enter the house but the sound of a car grabbed his attention. Loretta was pulling into the portico. Perfect timing. She killed the engine and he met her in time to open the car door for her.

"Evenin', Loretta. How's your friend?"

"She's struggling, but I think I cheered her up a bit. Thanks for asking, Cooper. Where's Lauren?"

"She just went for a walk. Did you get it?"

"I did. It's in the trunk." Loretta pushed a button and her trunk opened.

He helped Loretta out of the car and then walked around to pick up Tony's laptop. "Got it. I hope he doesn't have a secret pass code or anything."

"He does."

Cooper's shoulders slumped.

"But I know it." Loretta grinned. "My son trusted me with his passwords."

"That makes life a lot simpler."

"Yes. I hope you find something."

"Me, too."

Cooper sighed. A lot was riding on this. As soon as he got the goods on Kelsey, all of the deceit would be over. Lauren was a good woman. As good as they come. And she deserved a better man than Roger Kelsey.

Four

"Holy crap." Cooper glanced at the clock in his study. He'd been listening for Lauren while sitting at his desk searching her brother's laptop for clues and had lost track of time. She'd been on her walk for over an hour.

He picked up his phone and texted her just in case he'd missed hearing her come in. When she didn't answer, he locked the laptop in a drawer and made his way down the hall. Taking the stairs two at a time, he moved as quietly as his boots would allow, hoping to find Lauren safe and sound in her bedroom.

Her door was open and he popped his head inside. The room was empty.

Not good.

He debated half a second to tell Loretta, but he didn't want to alarm her.

Instead he made a beeline down the stairs and out the door that led to the garage. Lauren probably didn't have her phone with her. Not in those tight pants anyway, or he would've noticed.

She'd been getting under his skin lately. He'd been noticing *all* the appealing things about her.

Like her honeyed hair catching the morning sunlight.

And her smile, sometimes sweet, sometimes mischievous, yet always bright.

The cute way she nibbled her lip while pondering something.

Luckily, he'd also noticed the direction she'd begun walking in earlier.

Damn. He should've never let her go on that walk alone. Stupidly, he'd let his effort to distance himself from her get in the way of good sense.

Hopping in his Jeep, he took off toward the stables and corrals but found no sign of her. All of his crew had gone home, except for Buddy, a security guard who watched the premises.

"No, sir. I haven't seen her, Mr. Stone," he said.

"Okay, why don't you head out in the opposite direction? Call me immediately if you find her."

"Yes, sir."

Cooper continued at a slow pace, scouring the land with a flashlight as he drove deeper and deeper onto the property. His pulse racing, his gut churning, he sent up prayers for her safety. Somehow Lauren had become more important to him than he'd realized. The thought of her out there, possibly harmed and lost, made him a little frantic.

And he *never* got frantic.

He was just about ready to call Jared to enlist his help, when he spotted something quite a distance from the road. "Lauren, Lauren!"

"I'm here, Cooper," she called out.

Thank God. He bounded out of the Jeep, shone the light in her direction and ran for all he was worth. He found her sitting on the ground, holding her bloodied leg, and he immediately bent to his knees and grabbed her tight around the shoulders. She felt small and delicate in his arms.

"Oh, man, Laurie Loo."

He brushed his lips to her hair, a soft little peck that said he was damn grateful he'd found her. He hugged her longer than he probably should have, unable to let go of her so easily. She was soft and so sweet, looking up at him like he was a savior. His chest swelled. Was he feeling more for her than friendship? He pulled back carefully to look into her eyes. "What happened?"

"I got lost about half an hour ago. I thought I knew the way back, but it's so dark and everything looked so different. And then I practically face-planted on a big rock. I caught myself but not before putting a good gash on my leg."

That's when he noticed that her pants were ripped below the knee. The gash appeared long and angry. She'd stripped away the bottom half of her cotton tank top to wrap around the wound.

"There's a lot of blood," he said. "Does it hurt?"

"It stings. But it's not fractured and I stopped the bleeding, so I consider myself lucky."

There were no tears on her face, no panic. She knew how to handle herself in a crisis. "Lucky?" He shook his head. "I guarantee you won't feel lucky in the morning."

"And here I had this secret plan to beat your butt at jogging tomorrow."

He smiled. How could he not? Lauren was something else. "I'll take a rain check, honey. But for now, let me get you back home. Can you stand?"

"I think so," she said.

He offered his hand and she stood, hopping up on her good leg, while keeping the pressure off her injured one. He slid his other hand around the creamy-smooth band of exposed skin around her waist. It startled him how delicate and soft she felt. She leaned against him and wrapped her arm around his waist. They moved slowly, Cooper taking on most of her weight, his fingers splaying wide, reaching to just under the swell of her breasts.

Oh, man. An instant insane reaction zeroed in down past his navel. He imagined touching her breasts but that crazy thought fled his mind the second she began to tremble. He had to remind himself Lauren was engaged and could never be his.

He stopped walking. She'd lost a lot of blood tonight and her face was pale. She gazed at him helplessly.

"Forget this." On impulse, he scooped her up gently, one arm at her shoulders, the other beneath her knees. "Rope your arms around my neck," he told her.

She tugged at his neck and he repositioned her. "Better?" he asked.

She squeezed her eyes shut. "Much."

He handed her the flashlight. "Point us back to the Jeep."

"That I can do," she said, sounding apologetic.

Hell, he should be apologizing to her. "I should've never let you go out by yourself tonight. You told me you were buzzed."

"I was fine," she whispered breathlessly. "It was a stupid accident."

He started moving again, taking long, careful strides. "You're not familiar enough with the ranch to go traipsing around in the dark without a phone or a flashlight."

"I guess I wasn't thinking straight."

"I should've known that, too."

Her fingertips grazed his right cheek and he turned to her. They were inches apart, her face so close he could feel her breaths. "Cooper, it wasn't your fault," she said softly.

He wasn't going to argue the point anymore. He simply nodded and kept walking. When they reached the Jeep, he was very deliberate in his movements getting her into the passenger seat. "You all right?"

"I'm fine."

He reached inside to pull the seat belt strap for her, his forearm grazing her breasts. "Uh, sorry."

"No problem."

Glad *she* thought so. He made quick work of securing her belt and then took off his shirt and handed it to her. "Here, put this around you," he said. "It might get chilly on the ride back." Already the night air had cooled some.

"Thanks," she said, eyeing him in his ribbed T-shirt. "You're always taking care of me."

He was always undressing for her, but he didn't point that out. "You're like…my sister. It's my job."

She pursed her lips and, if he didn't know better, he'd think she was pouting.

"Does Roger take care of you?"

"Roger? Um, he knows I'm capable. He's—"

"Let me guess…always so busy."

"He is. But he's coming by tomorrow afternoon to help with the arrangements. I hope that's okay with you, Cooper."

"Sure." He gunned the engine and took off. There was no further talk of Roger.

Minutes later he pulled up to the house and opened the Jeep door for her.

"I can try to walk," Lauren said.

"Don't think so. You'll never make it up the stairs."

Her mouth opened and then closed. Whatever protest she had on her lips was left unsaid. He wasn't budging. He bent to lift her and adjusted her in his arms. He was getting used to the feel of her, the softness of her skin, her flowery scent. He carried her inside the house and up the stairs.

Loretta's bedroom door was shut, the light was off. She was probably asleep and there was no sense waking her. He moved down the hallway to Lauren's room and entered.

A sliver of moonlight filtered in, casting enough light for him to see where he was going. Cooper walked over to her bed. "I'm going to put you down now."

"Okay," she whispered.

He carefully released her and she slid down his body until her feet hit the floor. His groin tightened and he gritted his teeth. It was torture keeping his intentions pure around her. Suddenly, his best friend's little sis was testing his willpower. He couldn't give in to temptation.

But as she tried to apply pressure to her leg she wobbled and he was there to catch her. "Whoa."

She was in his arms again, leaning against his chest. "Are you in pain? Should I call a doctor?"

"No, Coop," she said, her head resting against his shoulder. "I'll take care of it. I'll redress the wound and clean it up a bit and then take some aspirin."

"What can I do?" he asked quietly.

"Help me into the bathroom. I'll…need some privacy to dress the wound."

"I can wake up your mom. She can help you."

"No, don't be silly. I'm an ER nurse, I've done this a thousand times."

"Fine. I'll hold on to you."

He helped her hobble into the bathroom and sit on a vanity chair. "I'll be right back. I have a first-aid kit in my room. Okay?"

"Okay."

He was back in thirty seconds and set the blue-and-white box on the counter. "Here you go. What else can I do?"

"I'm going to soak my leg a bit and then dress the wound. I have to get out of these pants."

She stared at him.

"I'm going. I'm going. But I'll be right outside the door if you need me."

She nodded and he left just as she started stripping out of her blood-soaked jeans.

He sat on her bed and waited what seemed like eons. He heard her moving around, the water in the tub being turned on and off. That was exactly how *he* felt, being constantly turned on by Lauren, and then trying like hell to turn it off. The problem was, it all felt so natural being around her. But she only saw him as a big brother figure and he couldn't very well disappoint her. Could he?

"Cooper? Are you still there?"

"I'm here."

"Please bring me my jammies. They're in the top right drawer in the dresser. They're blue."

Cooper found them right away, a silky blue top and a pair of pants to match. "Got them."

She opened the door and one hand came out to grab at them and haul them away. Then the door shut again. "Thanks."

A few minutes later she was standing against the open door in her sleek pajamas that fell over the contours of her body, the silk hiding very little of her form. She looked beautiful, so much better than when he'd found her bruised and disheveled earlier. Her face was beet-red, though. "This is embarrassing."

"It's not the first time I've seen you in pajamas," he

said, trying to hold on to her image as a kid and not think about the woman standing right in front of him.

She sighed. "That's true. But that had to be fifteen years ago or something."

"You dressed the wound?"

"Yes, and I took some meds. I think I'm going to live."

She hobbled over to him and he thought to back away. To keep his distance. But there was determination in her eyes and, man, he couldn't resist planting his boots and seeing what she had in mind.

"Thank you, Cooper," she whispered. "You've been wonderful."

She reached up on tiptoes to plant a sweet kiss on his cheek. But when she put weight on her bad leg, she stumbled. He caught her, holding her tight, his hands gripping her upper arms. Her eyes flashed, all that meadow green working magic on him. Holding her like this felt right—and that was all wrong. But when she dipped her gaze to his mouth, the longing in her eyes did him in.

"Cooper."

He put his hands in her hair and tilted her head up. Their eyes locked, wrecking his resistance, wrecking any semblance of rational thought. He brought his mouth down and touched his lips to hers.

It was Fourth of July fireworks and sweet cake on Sunday morning all rolled into one. She was soft and delicate and amazingly sexy. But one brush of the lips wasn't enough; he needed more, demanded more. She made little noises in the back of her throat and the sounds were like music and laughter and brightness. His body grew tight and hard and Lauren seemed just as lost, just as needy. She hugged his neck, ran her fingers through his hair and he deepened the kiss even more.

"Lauren?"

It was Loretta calling out from her room. He froze and stared at Lauren. She stared back, wide-eyed. She waited a beat and then said, "Y-yes, Mama?"

"Okay, just making sure you got home from your walk."

"I did, Mama. I'm in bed."

"Good night, sweetheart."

"'Night, Mama."

Cooper released her and ran a hand down his face. *Oh, man.*

Lauren seemed equally stunned.

"Cooper, what was that?" she asked so softly he could barely hear her.

"That was me, not being brotherly. Not being smart. God, I'm so sorry, Lauren. I was worried about you tonight and that was my relief coming out. That's all it was. I promise you."

"But, Cooper. That kiss was—"

"All wrong, Lauren. It was a mistake and I take all the blame."

"Blame? You're constantly blaming yourself for everything. I had something to do with that kiss, in case you didn't notice." She was whispering but her words rang loudly in his ears. He wasn't buying them. He couldn't.

"I noticed. But, no." He began shaking his head. "No. I got caught up in the moment is all. I'm sorry and I hope you can forgive me."

With that, he strode quietly out of her room.

Heading straight for the bar and a double shot of whiskey.

The good stuff.

Lauren sat up in bed and rubbed her temples. She hadn't gotten much sleep last night. The ache in her leg and the memory of kissing Cooper—just the way she'd fantasized as a young girl—made her fuzzy-brained. It was an awesome kiss, filled with passion, filled with heat. He was a take-charge kind of guy and he'd certainly taken charge of the situation last night. Being in Cooper's arms had been heavenly. And that kiss, though way too brief, had blown her mind. Cooper's reaction told her it was good for him, too.

What had provoked it? He'd said it was over his concern for her. That, she believed. But could it be more? No one had ever kissed her like that before. Not even Roger.

She chewed on her bottom lip. She shouldn't be comparing the two men. Roger was her fiancé. She was planning their wedding. And last night with Cooper was just a fluke. Something he said wouldn't happen again. She had to believe him. Didn't she?

Strong midmorning sunlight poured in through the shutters and warmed her skin. The day had begun without her. Maybe it was a good thing she'd missed breakfast. How would she react when she saw Cooper today? It would be weird, that was for sure.

She swung her legs over the edge of the bed and her feet hit the floor. Putting slight pressure on her injured leg to test it, she rose. There was no pain that made her wince, thank goodness, just a dull ache that would fade with time and pain meds. The gash wasn't deep enough for stitches, but it was long and ugly. Still, not as bad as it could've been.

Thirty minutes later, after washing up and dressing, she was ready to face the day. She limped to the window and looked out on the ranch, which was already bustling with activity. There was a soft rapping at her door. Her mama was probably wondering why she had overslept and missed breakfast.

"Mama, I'll be right there."

She limped to the door and opened it.

"Not your mama," Cooper said, briefly smiling. Surprised, all she could do was stare into his blue, blue eyes. Dressed in jeans and a crisp, tan shirt, he stood tall in the doorway, concern on his face.

"No, I can see that." She gulped air.

"I came to check on you. How's the leg?"

"Better. The pain is manageable and I'm walking… well, limping. I'll be fine, Cooper."

"Good to hear." He sighed and rubbed the back of his neck. "Listen, about last night."

She froze. He wanted to talk about the kiss? In the light of day? She braced herself against the doorjamb.

"I don't want things to be awkward between us, Lauren. What happened was about me being worried."

"So you said last night."

"It's the truth. I hope you and I can put this past us. We're friends. I don't want to ruin that."

"No, I don't, either, Coop."

He smiled and a shot of heat warmed her up inside. Apparently he liked it when she used his nickname. She had to remember not to do that again. "Okay, then. We're good?"

She nodded. It was in both of their best interests to lock that kiss up and toss the key away. "Yeah, we're good. Of course."

"I'm really glad you're feeling better."

"Thanks."

"Oh, and when your mother came down to breakfast, I explained what happened…about you getting hurt. She was concerned but wanted you to rest. She's downstairs now, cooking up your favorite breakfast. If you don't go down, she'll probably come up and check on you."

"Sure, I'll go down."

"Need help with the stairs?"

Thinking about him touching her again after that kiss put fear in her heart. The good kind of fear, that thrilled and excited and immediately an image of Roger nestled into her brain. Goodness, she'd almost forgotten about him. What a terrible fiancée she was. "No, thanks. I can manage."

He stared at her a moment, the handsome planes of his face immovable. It was hard not to get caught up in that stare. "Okay, then," he rasped. "Have a good day, Lauren."

She took a big swallow. "Thanks. Same to you."

He walked away and after she closed the door she pressed her back up against it.

Boy, that conversation was weird and *awkward*. Maybe it was just her. She'd have to get over it. She had enough on her plate right now. And her dear Roger was coming out to the ranch this afternoon.

She smiled. Once she saw him, she'd get her head on straight.

Cooper locked himself up in the study and concentrated on the files on Tony's laptop. He wasn't a numbers man and all the accounts looked in order. But then, he wouldn't know it if a big fat discrepancy jumped up to bite him in the ass. He had no clue what he was looking for. The files were massive, with contracts and conditions and specs for new building projects as well as the ones they'd already completed. Real-estate development was more complicated than the running of a ranch. Maybe he hadn't given his buddy enough credit for his smarts.

After two hours of digging, Cooper found a folder named Family. Clicking on it, he leaned back in his chair and smiled as pictures came up of the Abbotts. Of course, Tony would keep photos of his family on his personal computer. They'd meant a lot to him. He eyed a photo of the whole Abbott family: a young Loretta with her husband David, Tony and a pip-squeak Lauren, smiling into the camera on their front doorstep. He was guessing Tony was probably twelve and little Lauren was about six when the photo was taken.

He clicked on the next batch of photos and watched the family evolve before his eyes. Lauren in grade school. Tony playing football, graduating middle school. Christmas. Easter. Fourth of July.

His own scrawny face popped up in some of those photos. He shook his head, laughing at himself. "You were one skinny dude, Cooper," he muttered.

He'd forgotten some of those moments, but their documentation brought everything racing back to his mind and he found himself smiling and missing his best friend. Some days it was so bad he'd absently reach for his phone to call his buddy and then it'd hit him all over again. Tony was gone.

"I'm trying," he said to a photo of the two of them sitting inside their fort. "Trying to find the truth. Trying to help Lauren."

He clicked on another photo in the folder labeled Lauren's Nursing School Graduation. And there she was in her pristine nursing uniform, a little cap on her head, looking serious with a proud gleam in her eyes.

"Beautiful," he murmured.

Kissing her had been crazy, but he'd never expected to react to her with so much heat. Hot need had poured through his veins once he'd tasted her and, heaven help him, where that kiss would've taken them if Loretta, calling from the other room, hadn't interrupted them. He shivered at the notion.

Lauren had participated fully, too. She'd been giving and generous, soft in his arms and… No, he didn't want to think about it. She was forbidden to him. And, damn, if that didn't test his strength. He'd given up women after Tony's death and he wasn't about to break his own vow with the one person he was trying damn hard to protect.

One thing was certain: he wasn't going to seduce her away from Roger. That notion had never crossed his mind when he'd come up with this plan. Especially now, after kissing her—a kiss he couldn't take back—he was even more determined to get the goods on Kelsey as quickly as possible.

He was ready to click out of the pictures folder when another subdirectory caught his eye. Uncle Bucky. As far as he knew there was no Uncle Bucky in the Abbott family. It was a code word he and Tony used as kids. When their roughhousing got out of hand, one of them would call "Uncle" and the other would say "Uncle who?"

Uncle Bucky meant stop at all costs.

Cooper clicked on the folder and another subfolder popped up.

Winding Hills Resort.

The name rang a bell. Tony had mentioned it before he'd died.

This might be exactly what Cooper was looking for.

Lauren sat at the kitchen table writing out her wedding invitations. She had pretty handwriting; at least that's what she'd been told by her friends who often asked her to do the invitations for special occasions. She'd helped with invites for Katy's brother's swearing-in party when he became an officer with the Dallas police department, as well as a few other friends who were getting married. She didn't mind doing it. It sort of felt like therapy, and just knowing she was helping her friends made it all worthwhile.

She concentrated on each envelope, keeping her lines straight, her letters even. Halfway through the stack, her mother came into the room, her shoulders slumped, worry lines around her eyes making her look ten years older.

Lauren stood from the table, her heart in her throat. "Mama, what's wrong?"

"It's Sadie, honey. She's had a stroke." Her mom began shaking her head. "I knew something wasn't right with her. She wasn't herself. She was all alone in that big house when it happened. Good thing the mailman was delivering a package to her door and heard her calling out."

Tears dripped down her mother's face. "I just got off the phone with her doctor's office. I was on her emergency contact list. Honey, I know the timing is bad, but I have to go see her."

"Of course, Mama. Of course. Do you want me to drive you?"

"No, sweetheart. Don't stop what you're doing. You've got a hundred details to get to and I'm only sorry I can't be here today to help with your invitations like I promised."

"It's okay, Mama. I've got everything under control. And Roger's coming out today. So, I'll have his help. You go on." She hugged her mother, giving her a big squeeze. "I love you, Mama."

"I love you, too, honey."

That's when she noticed the luggage sitting in the kitchen doorway. "Are you staying overnight?"

"Oh, I think I'll have to. I don't know how long I'll be, honey. It depends. Sadie's only son is stationed overseas. With him being a career soldier, who knows when he can get back to see his mother. She doesn't have anyone else but me."

"I know, Mama. She needs you. And I've got Katy and Roger to help me."

"All right." Her mother sighed. "I'll be on my way now. If you're sure."

"I'm sure."

"And your leg? How's it feeling this afternoon?"

"Better. It's just ugly, but the pain's almost gone. Don't worry about me. You just be careful." She kissed her mother's smooth cheek. At sixty-two, her mother still had soft and supple skin. Hopefully those good genes would be passed down to her.

Being a nurse all those years had kept her mother fit and toned, too. They said you never got over being a nurse. The nurturer inside always came through. For her mother, that was certainly the case.

"Here, let me see you out," she said.

She picked up the suitcase and walked her mother to the car. Her sore leg was healing; she was barely limping now and that was a good thing. She stowed the luggage in the trunk and kissed her mother one last time before sending her off. After watching her pull away, Lauren lifted her face to the sun. The rays beat down, soaking into her skin, announcing the coming of June.

Images of her wedding day by the lake poured into

her mind. She hoped for a beautiful day like today to speak her vows. She hoped for everything to go smoothly.

"Your mama going somewhere?"

Startled, she jumped and spun around to face Cooper. She pushed at his chest. "You scared the dickens out of me."

His chest was granite and he remained immobile, except for the wide grin spreading across his smug mug. "Sorry."

He didn't sound sorry. "Where did you come from?"

"I've been locked away in my study. Working. You didn't answer my question. Where's your mama going?"

"Our neighbor Sadie had a stroke this morning. Mama went to sit with her at the hospital."

"That's rough."

"Yeah, it is."

"I noticed you putting her luggage in the trunk."

"She doesn't think she'll make it back tonight." And then it dawned on her: she would be alone with Cooper in his big, beautiful house. "But Roger's coming," she blurted. Yes, things were definitely weird between her and Cooper since that kiss. "He should be here in an hour or two."

Cooper nodded. "Okay. Well, then, I guess I'll see you later. I'm heading over to my brother's right now."

"Okay. Tell Jared I said hello."

"Will do."

With that, she entered the house and headed straight for the kitchen to finish addressing her invitations.

Tomorrow morning they'd go out in the mail and that would be one more thing she could cross off her list. She was making progress.

By three o'clock, she was done. Her cell phone rang and she picked up right away. "Hi, Katy."

"Hey. How's it going? This is the maid of honor daily call."

"It's going good. Got the invitations all done. But I, uh, got a little hurt last night."

"What does that mean? How hurt?"

"It's not too bad and it should heal in time for the wedding."

"It's gonna take three more weeks to heal? What on earth did you do?"

Lauren took a minute to give Katy the details about her stumble in the dark.

"So, hunky Cooper came to your rescue? Did he carry you up the stairs and into your bedroom?" Katy joked and when Lauren paused overly long to answer, a loud gasp resounded through the phone line. "He did. He pulled a Rhett Butler?"

"I couldn't walk and, yes, he carried me up the stairs."

"Oh, man, to be a fly on that wall."

"Nothing…happened. Uh, much."

"What does 'uh, much' mean?"

"You know how much I love Roger, right?"

"Yeah, I do. He makes you happy and that's all I care about. So…what aren't you telling me?"

"It's just that…well, Cooper kissed me last night. But he claimed it was only a nervous reaction because

I scared him when he couldn't find me and…well, he was worried sick about me."

"And what did you do?" Katy asked.

She sighed, recalling the mind-numbing kiss that had ended way too early. "I kissed him back."

Katy's "wow" was less than a whisper.

"It's just that…you know I've had an on-and-off crush on Cooper since forever. So, I indulged. Out of curiosity. That's all it was."

"Because the kiss was lousy, right? Tell me it wasn't any good."

"Okay, yes, it was a…lousy kiss." She might go straight to hell with that lie.

"Liar."

There was no fooling her bestie.

"Because just on general principles alone, a guy as hot as Cooper Stone would definitely be a good kisser," Katy persisted.

She didn't want to think about it.

"Lauren?"

"Hmm?"

"What are you doing?"

She had no clue. She wasn't even sure why she'd told Katy about kissing Cooper. It wasn't as if anything was going to happen. Cooper had said it himself. It was a mistake. And she had to agree with him.

"What I'm doing is waiting for Roger. He's due here any minute."

"Okay, good." Her friend sighed in relief. And Lauren felt better about everything, too. Roger would make things right.

"I almost forgot the reason I called. That country band I told you about has a weekend gig starting this Friday night in a little honky-tonk in town. Maybe you and Roger could check it out."

"That's a great idea. Thanks, Katy. The best maid of honor ever."

"Yeah, I'm getting the hang of this. It's fun. And I'm emailing you a list of caterers I found. I think you'll find someone on there you can use for the wedding dinner."

"Perfect."

The doorbell chimed and Lauren instantly rose. "Someone's at the door. I think Roger's here. I'd better go."

"Tell him I said hello. 'Bye, Lauren."

"'Bye, Katy."

Lauren straightened out her clothes. She'd meant to change from her slacks into a dress, but her wound wasn't a pretty sight. And Roger had complimented her once on this pale sage blouse. Taking a look at herself in the foyer mirror, she finger-combed her hair and then went to the door. Taking a deep breath, she opened it. "Roger, I'm so glad you're here."

"I made it." He removed his sunglasses, looking very *GQ* standing there in a slate suit and charcoal tie. He bent to give her a peck on the cheek. "This place is quite a drive from civilization."

"It's just twenty miles from town. And it's beautiful here. Come inside." She took his hand and led him into the parlor. "I can't wait to show you everything."

"Yeah, about that. We have to make it quick. I've got an early flight out tomorrow morning."

"Tomorrow?"

"Yes, at 8:00 a.m. I'm right in the middle of this big project, Lauren. And I've got meetings in Houston and San Antonio."

"But I have a lot to talk to you about."

He gave her hand a squeeze. "I know, but we were supposed to have a small wedding, babe. Remember? I told you, if you wanted to do this, you'd be pretty much on your own. And I'm here now, so show me what you want to show me. I can stay a couple of hours."

"Just a couple?"

Her disappointment didn't seem to unsettle him. He smiled, showing off pearly white teeth and distracting twin dimples. Cradling her in his arms, he murmured, "Yes, and I can think of better things to do with you than go over wedding plans."

She pursed her lips. Going to bed was Roger's answer to settling their disputes. Not that this was a dispute or anything, but right now, his charm wasn't working on her. Their wedding plans were important and even though he'd told her he couldn't get involved in the details, she'd thought he'd be around more to give his opinion on things.

"Roger, it's just that I thought we could have dinner and spend some time together."

"We will, Lauren. Once I get back from this trip next week."

"You're leaving town *for a week*?"

He sighed and shook his head. "Lauren, after we're

married, we'll have a ton of time together. You know this project is important. It's something Tony and I worked on together. And now the brunt of the work has fallen on me."

"Sorry my brother's death gave you a heavier work-load."

She squeezed her eyes shut. *Oh, man.* Had she re-ally said that? Was she resentful of Roger because he put his work ahead of their wedding plans or was she still hurting because her brother wasn't there to build his company as he'd always dreamed?

"You don't mean that," Roger said. "You know Tony wasn't just my partner, he was a friend. I'm only try-ing to hang on to the company we built. For Tony as much as for us."

A knot formed in the pit of her stomach. She felt small and ridiculous for suggesting such a thing. Of course, Roger was working super hard doing the work of two men, trying to hold on to the deals that were made while Tony was alive. She was a partner in the company now and had no knowledge of what went on there. She had her own career. Roger was taking it on all by himself. For both of them.

"I'm sorry," she said. "I really didn't mean it. I shouldn't have said that."

She didn't understand why she'd blurted it out, but Roger smiled after her apology. He didn't hold a grudge and he understood she was still grieving for her brother.

"Are you going to show me that lake now?"

"Yes, of course. It's just a ways down the road. And this is the perfect time of day to see it."

Exactly two hours passed. After showing Roger the lake, and being given a lukewarm okay to hold the wedding there, she also discussed the possibilities of caterers and bands with him and showed him his own wedding invitation. She'd texted him a picture of it, but at least now he'd seen it firsthand. Not too much else had been decided from their talk and now her allotted time with him was up. She stood next to Roger by his midnight-blue Cadillac.

"You're doing a great job, Lauren. I've got faith in you," he said.

She didn't want to be a Debbie Downer, so she gave him a smile. "Thanks. I'm doing my best. I hope it's good enough."

"It'll be fine." He sounded dismissive. As if, as if… he really didn't care. They could have just as easily been talking about what movie they would see next, for all his enthusiasm. But she wanted more than fine. She wanted to start her married life off with fireworks, not a caution sign. And Roger was definitely sucking the joy out of her wedding plans.

"Hey," he said, tilting his head and eyeing her. "Don't pout. Although, on you it's kind of cute." He glanced at his watch. "Oh, damn. I've gotta run. I have to pack and put together my agenda for the next week. Sorry, babe."

"It's okay. I get it. Have a good trip, Roger."

"Will do." Then he pulled her into his arms and kissed her solidly on the lips. His hand slid through her hair and she was momentarily lost. But his kiss didn't have the usual impact. She was miffed at him, but when Roger finally broke it off, he didn't pick up on her mood.

Or if he did, he was in too much of a rush to deal with it. Or her. "I'll call you," he said. "I promise."

"Okay. Talk to you soon."

After he pulled away, she stood there on the walkway a few moments until his car was out of sight. Then she turned toward the house and found Cooper standing on the veranda, his arms folded across his chest, his blue gaze pinned on her, as if he'd been there a long while. He looked rugged and solid, the scruff on his face more attractive than he could ever know. The contrast between Roger and Cooper wasn't hard to notice. *GQ* versus *Modern Cowboy*. City versus country.

An unexpected queasiness settled in her belly. And the reason pounded in her skull. Roger had ticked her off and now Cooper was there. Making her heart do little tiny flips.

Wow. She couldn't go there. Ever again. She'd *flipped* over too many guys in her past and that phase of her life was dead and buried. She wasn't a boy-crazy young girl anymore. She had a reputation of being fickle and indecisive to live down. Not just for her family and friends, but for herself, too. She'd outgrown her silly crushes and fantasies. She wasn't going to allow herself any notions about Cooper Stone.

Not when she had a good, stable fiancé to love.

She put up her hand and waved to Cooper. "Sorry you missed Roger."

He nodded and pivoted around, walking into the house.

The door shut behind him. Kind of hard.

Had he just slammed the door on her?

Five

Locked in his study again, Cooper was pissed and anxious and frustrated. Seeing Roger kissing Lauren goodbye ticked him off on too many levels. It'd been hard to watch. He ground his teeth together; at this rate, he'd have those back teeth worn down to a nub in no time.

The look on Lauren's face after Kelsey had left the ranch was stamped in his mind. The guy couldn't spare her more than a few hours? He was a jerk and wasn't fit to touch Lauren, much less marry her. One glance at her sad face when she'd turned to Cooper tugged at something deep inside. His anger boiled over to an emotion far more dangerous…jealousy. It was a sharp knife twisting in his heart. She deserved much better.

After an hour of going over inventory, Cooper

shoved away from his desk and stared out the window. It was dark now. The sun had set a short time ago and there wasn't much to see. He sighed and picked up his cell, pushing his brother's number on speed dial.

"Hey, didn't I just see you a couple hours ago?" Jared said.

"Did you get a chance to look over those files?"

His brother laughed. "Are you serious? You dropped off the laptop—what?—three hours ago. I haven't looked at anything yet."

"Okay. Gotcha. I was hoping something glaring would stick out, is all. Something I overlooked."

"Maybe, but doubtful. Things don't work like that. It could take days, bro, if I find anything at all, so don't get your panties in a knot. You need patience, Coop."

Cooper ground his teeth again. "Yeah, that's not so easy. I don't have a lot of time. Lauren is…making a mistake."

"Yeah, I know. But unfortunately it's hers to make. I don't suppose you're getting in too deep?"

"What the hell does that mean?"

"It means, are you doing this for Lauren and Tony or for yourself?"

"Myself?"

"I've never seen you so invested in a…woman. You're chomping at the bit on this one."

"Fact is, I stuck my nose in and now I have to follow through, Jared. What was I supposed to do when Loretta came to me? I couldn't refuse her. And now that I know, or think I know, what this guy is up to, I can't drop it."

"So you don't have feelings for Lauren?"

"No."

"Okay, just checking. Because remember what happened between me and Helene. I don't want that to happen to you."

"It won't. Helene was lying to you the whole time."

"Just like you're lying through your teeth with Lauren."

"That's different."

"The fact is, I thought it was a casual thing until it wasn't. I was in over my head with her," Jared said, a bit of longing in his voice.

"She broke your heart."

"She used me and, yeah, broke my heart. I've been over Helene for a while now. I'm more cautious and I don't get involved with women much anymore. But you're the one I'm worried about. You're deceiving Lauren and when she finds out, this won't end well."

"Hopefully, it won't come to that. Hopefully, you'll find something on the computer."

"No pressure or anything, bro."

"Hey, what am I supposed to do?"

"Butt out."

"It's too late for that. I'm worried about Lauren and Loretta. I couldn't stand it if these women get taken by Kelsey. Even if Lauren winds up hating me, she'll eventually come to realize I was only trying to save her and her company. She's got almost blind trust in Kelsey and I don't trust the guy. I know this is a big favor…"

"I'm on it," Jared said.

Cooper ended the conversation and strode out of

the study. What he needed was to blow off steam. Let the weights and incline treadmill kick his ass and rid him of restless energy. He entered the gym with that in mind.

An hour later and totally wiped out, Cooper felt better. Nothing like a hard workout to clear the head. He entered the shower and hot steam immediately soaked into his abused muscles. He finished up with a shocking spray of cool water and then dried off.

Refreshed, he exited the shower area and came face-to-face with Lauren.

Her eyes widened and her lips parted. Her surprised expression probably mirrored his own. "Oh, I'm so sorry."

Her gaze dipped down to the towel wrapped around his waist. The only thing he had on. She swallowed hard, blinked and looked back up at his bare chest. A warm gleam entered her eyes.

Dang it. Why'd he have to go and notice things like that? He forced a smile. But he was noticing more than her eyes. Her neon-pink bikini, for one, caught his attention, as well as the luscious swells of her breasts, her flat, toned stomach and all that creamy, exposed skin. Before he could get more than a glimpse, she hoisted her towel up like a shield of protection.

"Don't be sorry," he managed to say, the sound more like a croak.

"I didn't mean to disturb you. I was going to soak in the indoor spa for a few minutes. For…my leg."

It was too late not to be disturbed. She was hot. And sexy. And sweet.

He secured the twist of towel at his waist and tried to think about cow dung to keep his body from reacting to her. With no real barrier but his towel, she might easily figure out where his thoughts were heading if he wasn't careful. "Be my guest."

"But, uh, are you sure? You're done in here?"

So done. "Yeah."

He gave her leg a glance. It looked better; the color was coming back. She should heal just fine. "I think it's a good idea."

"Thanks. I'll just go…" she said, backing away from him. As if…as if she was thinking the same thoughts he was. Any awkwardness they felt couldn't compete with the edgy desire floating in the air. It was scary.

"What happened with Roger?" he blurted. It wasn't as if he wanted to prolong their conversation, but he had to know what was going on between the two of them.

"He likes the lake for the ceremony."

"Good. He didn't stay too long."

"No, he had business. He's going to be gone a week."

The son of a bitch. Cooper kept still, holding back a reaction.

"It's just inconvenient," she continued. "I was hoping we could…never mind. You don't want to hear all this. I'll manage."

Her meek tone of disappointment singed his nerves.

"Hey, have you had dinner yet?"

"No, I wasn't too hungry before."

"Marie left us tamale pie. I was going to have some out on the pool deck. Want to join me later?"

She hugged the towel tighter, so it covered up all her lush parts. He was partially insane for inviting her to dinner so late at night, but the sane part of him wanted to put a smile back on her face.

"Sure," she said. "I'll meet you outside…say, at nine?"

"Yeah, nine is good. You go on and enjoy the spa."

"Okay, thanks again." She turned, still tightly clutching the towel to her front.

But he got a sweet view of her ass and the soft folds of skin that didn't quite make it into her bikini bottoms as she walked away.

The dim overhead light, clink of utensils and laughter and shouts of noisy patrons gave the honky-tonk the ambience it needed to draw a small crowd for open mic weekend. The band Lauren came here to see was about to play. Her partner in crime, Katy, had come down with a stomach bug suddenly, leaving Lauren in the lurch tonight.

Her eyes touched upon Cooper, her stand-in fiancé, who looked every bit the part of a swoon-worthy cowboy in a black felt hat, snap-down, blue-plaid shirt and crisp new jeans. He'd been a good sport about taking her tonight. Not that she'd asked. He'd insisted. A woman alone in the Dallas Palace meant one thing—getting hit upon over and over—and he'd offered to spare her that complication. So here they were.

"Want another beer?" he asked from across their café-size table.

"Sure," she said. Why not be adventurous?

Cooper caught the attention of their very blonde, very buxom waitress and lifted two fingers her way. She gave him a nod and if that coy wink was accidental, Lauren would eat his hat. She'd noticed the attention Cooper drew from female eyes the second they'd walked into the place. She had no right or reason to be jealous.

Heavens no.

Yet a sharp pang kept jabbing at her belly every time a woman eyed her…friend.

She certainly hadn't had friendly thoughts about him last night in the gym. Not when she'd practically stripped him bare with her eyes. It hadn't been too hard, considering he'd been nearly naked at that point. The image of his powerful shoulders and chest ripped with muscles would haunt her for a long time.

But everything had gotten back to normal during their tamale pie dinner. Dressed casually and in a more subdued frame of mind, they'd simply relaxed on the patio deck and had quiet conversation over a delicious meal.

"I'm surprised you're not drinking whiskey," she said over the din of conversation surrounding them.

"Love to. But I need to keep my wits about me."

"I can drive home, Coop. If that's what you're getting at."

His gaze dipped to her mouth before he met her eyes.

Goose bumps erupted on her arms and a wave of heat filled her stomach. Maybe that's not what he meant at all.

"Yeah. Designated driver and all that."

Pulse racing, she nibbled on her lower lip, not quite sure if he was telling the truth. But just then Westward Movement took the stage and she sighed, relieved.

"There they are. Katy says they can play any kind of music and the vocalist is pretty good."

"We'll find out soon enough."

"Yes, we will. Before they go on, I think I'll use the ladies' room."

Cooper stood and pulled her chair out.

"Thanks."

She bumped a few shoulders on her way to the restroom at the back of the club. When she was done, she hesitated by the back wall.

It was Saturday night and she hadn't heard from Roger all day. On impulse, she dialed his cell phone number. She thought it odd when he didn't answer. Next, she called the hotel and asked to be connected to his room. After the first ring, a female voice answered. "I hope you're calling about our dinner. We ordered over an hour ago and we're starving."

"Uh, hello?"

"Is this room service?"

"No, this is Lauren Abbott. Who are you?"

There was a pause. Her pulse pounded as a few more seconds ticked by. "Oh, Lauren. Hi. I'm sorry. This is Roger's secretary, Pam. How are you?"

"Pam?"

Auburn-haired divorcée Pam Hutton was on the trip with her fiancé? This she did not know.

There was noise in the background and then Roger's voice boomed in her ear. "Lauren, hello, sweetheart."

"Roger? What's going on?"

"Nothing, why?"

"Because you…well, you didn't tell me Pam was going on the trip with you."

"You make it sound like a vacation. We're working."

"Working? It's almost ten o'clock on Saturday night."

"We're busy, honey. We've been working so hard, we almost forgot to eat dinner. Don't tell me you're jealous? You know you don't have anything to be worried about. I'm doing this for us. For you and me."

"Still, Roger. I was surprised to hear her pick up the phone."

"Hey, I know. But…trust me. As soon as we eat, we're calling it quits. I have an early morning meeting tomorrow."

"On Sunday?"

"Yes, I'm meeting with the mayor of Houston for breakfast. If all goes well, the project will be approved. Tony would be pleased. Winding Hills Resort was originally his idea."

That was odd. She remembered it the other way around. Tony didn't think Winding Hills Resort was a good idea. He'd said they weren't ready for such a massive project. There was way too much risk involved and it could bankrupt the company if anything went wrong. But Roger had been pressuring him about it.

"It was? I thought Tony was against it?"

"No, you've got that wrong, sweetheart. Listen, I'm beat. How about we discuss it when I get back?"

"Okay." But by then it could be too late. She sighed. What did she know about real-estate development, anyway? Roger was the expert.

"Good night, sweetheart. Love ya."

"I love you…too."

He hung up first and she stood there with the cell phone to her ear, her stomach queasy. Rapid thoughts fired through her head and she shook them off. She trusted Roger. He'd given her no reason not to and, besides, if he'd asked, she would've told him she was out having drinks with Cooper Stone at a honky-tonk. Innocent as it was, her fiancé might have gotten the wrong idea, too.

That settled, she returned to her table and to Cooper.

The band began playing a cover of a Lady Antebellum song, about needing and wanting in the middle of the night. The vocalist brought the message home with grinding clarity, the tune touching deep into Lauren's soul. When she glanced at Cooper, his attention wasn't on the music. It was on her.

"Everything okay?" His blue gaze caressed her face, calming her.

"Everything's good." Looking at him made it so.

Rising from the table, Cooper offered her his hand. "Dance with me, Lauren."

This was a mistake. A horrible mistake. But an image of Roger and Pam having a late-night dinner in a hotel room surged into her head and she grasped Cooper's hand, eagerly following him onto the dance floor.

It was awkward at first, with Cooper holding her at arm's length, but surprisingly his footsteps and fluid moves on the parquet floor eased the tension as he led her into twirl after twirl. They circled the space, laughing and grinning.

The vocalist's beautiful tone resonated in her ears and the band solidly hit every note. Patrons bumped into her, their bodies crowding her on the floor, and soon she was pushed closer and closer into Cooper's arms. He took it all in stride, never missing a beat, and the room seemed to wind out of control as she spun around and around.

When the song ended, beads of sweat drizzled down her forehead. She wiped at them with the back of her arm, completely disregarding feminine etiquette. Cooper's forehead was moist, too. Up close, his musky scent bombarded her senses.

He leaned over and spoke into her ear. "Want to sit down?"

She shook her head. She hadn't had this much fun in a long time. "Not unless you're plum tired out," she drawled, mocking his stamina.

He raised an eyebrow, meeting her challenge. "Not on your life."

To her dismay, Westward Movement chose that time to play a sentimental ballad. But both of them refused to back down. Texans didn't shy away from a gauntlet thrown.

Again, Cooper kept her at a safe distance and they moved fluidly around the dance floor. The song was much slower than the one before. She shuffled her feet, matching Cooper's pace, and their bodies edged closer and closer as if magnetically drawn to each other.

Cooper's raspy voice reached her ears. "How does it feel being Roger's business partner now?" he asked out of the blue.

She blinked her eyes. "I don't know. It doesn't feel like anything really."

"So, you haven't gotten involved in Kelsey-Abbott?"

"No, not really. I leave all that up to Roger. Why do you ask?"

"Just wondering if the ER nurse is ever going to make it as a real-estate mogul."

She laughed. "Hardly. I can't read a contract for beans, but I sure as hell can read a medical chart."

Cooper nodded, and she got lost in the music again. As the soulful song continued, their legs brushed, her arms wound around his neck and her head rested on his chest. Her ears filled not with the music but with the steady and rapid beats of his heart. Wrapped up in Cooper, she lost sight of everything else. That couldn't be a good thing, but each breath they shared, each step they took, each innocent touch of their bodies, called to her and made her think stray thoughts.

Dear Lord.

She didn't dare look into his eyes.

She heard him swallow.

Scolding herself, she begged for mercy. She had to find a way out of this growing fascination she had for Cooper. She was done allowing her fickle mind to rule her destiny. She wasn't falling for Cooper Stone.

She couldn't.

She wouldn't.

She lifted her head from his rock-solid chest to tell him that very thing. To break away from his hold and to get a grip on her silly emotions. But one look into the blue blaze of his eyes and she was lost. Totally and unbelievably lost. The image of Roger she tried pulling up faded away like a speck of sand carried in the wind, and all she could see right now was this fine, magnificent man.

"Lauren," he rasped as he halted his steps. Taking her chin and lifting her face closer to his, his mouth came down slowly, giving her an out, giving her time to back away. But she was locked in, connecting to him as she had no other man. Feeling his desire underneath the belt buckle of his jeans wasn't helping.

His rough, rugged intensity captivated her. He was a man's man. A man any woman would want. And he was ready to kiss her again. And she...she didn't have the willpower to stop him.

He must have seen the turmoil in her eyes and then the final acceptance. He wasted not a moment. The man of action claimed her mouth, brushing his lips over hers, igniting a spark in her that flamed from the initial touch.

She hugged his neck harder, tighter, and he groaned deep in his throat. The kiss intensified and the first stroke of his tongue against hers sent her spiraling. Little moans erupted from her mouth as she kissed him back and settled into the luscious scent and taste of him.

Luckily, they didn't stand out in the smoky, crowded

room. They weren't making a spectacle of themselves. But she could feel his arousal against her belly. She could hardly believe that Cooper Stone wanted her this way. He was, and had always been...unreachable.

But in the moment, she was his.

And it scared the life out of her.

The song ended and so did the kiss. They parted and stood facing each other on the dance floor, staring into each other's eyes. Cooper didn't try to explain it away. He didn't say it was a mistake. He just stood there, eyes gleaming, touching her even though there was no longer a physical connection.

"Miss Abbott?" a young-sounding man called out behind her. She swiveled around.

The guitarist with long brown hair from the band was smiling at her and she had to blink several times to rejoin reality. "Yes, I'm Lauren Abbott."

"Nice to meet you." He put out his hand and she took it. "I'm Jodie's cousin, Stevie Johnston. Jodie told me you might be interested in our band playing at your wedding." He turned to Cooper. "And you must be the lucky groom?" He put out his hand. "Stevie Johnston."

"Oh, no. He's not the groom," she blurted. "He's a... friend. Cooper Stone."

Cooper shook the guy's hand. "Nice meeting you."

Stevie eyed the two of them and blinked, passing off any confusion he might've had. "Same here. No pressure or anything, but if there's a song you'd like to hear us play during our next set, we'd be happy to accommodate you."

"Oh…um. No, that's not necessary," she said. "I think…you're a good fit. Your band is really good."

"Thanks. We try."

"Just curious. How did you know who I was?"

He grinned. "You probably don't remember me, but I was a patient of yours a few years ago. You treated me in the emergency room and I never forgot you. You were like an angel from Heaven, holding my hand while I cried my eyes out, thinking I might be dying. I was eighteen at the time and had crashed my motorcycle."

Lauren didn't remember. She'd treated too many accident victims to recall them all, but she wouldn't tell Stevie that. "I was just doing my job and I'm glad I could help you."

"You told me to give up motorcycles and follow my true path."

"Music?"

"Yeah, and as you can see, I took your advice."

She smiled.

"Jodie tells me you're still a nurse. That's a good thing."

"Thanks for saying that. It means a lot to me."

"Well, here's how you can reach me, if you're interested." He took a card out of his jean jacket pocket and handed it to her.

"Stevie, I'm glad you're doing well and, yes, I will definitely be giving you a call."

"Cool. Nice meeting you both," he said and then turned and walked back toward the stage.

Lauren headed for their table. The business card in

her hand reminded her she was getting married in less than three weeks and had come there to hire a band for the wedding, yet all she could think about was Cooper and that hot kiss they'd just shared.

"I think we should go," she said to Cooper, fidgeting with her purse, refusing to look at him.

"Yeah," he said quietly. "Let's get out of here."

He didn't take her hand or offer his arm.

She had no clue what was going on inside his head.

Or, for that matter, what was going on in hers.

But she was about to find out.

Six

The dark moonless night made the drive from Dallas with Cooper intense. A grating silence sliced the air. Cooper drove down the highway, his foot heavy on the pedal, the wheels of his SUV quickly eating up the asphalt.

Lauren's phone rang, the sudden sound nearly making her jump out of her seat. A photo of her mama's smiling face stared at her from the screen. She assembled her wayward thoughts and answered her cell. "Mama? Is everything all right?"

"No, dear. I'm sorry to say Sadie had another stroke. It's a mild one, but the doctors are concerned and I can't leave her side. She's going in and out, and it puts her mind at ease when she wakes up and sees me here.

I wanted you to know I won't be coming back to the ranch tonight. Maybe not for a few more nights."

"Oh, I'm so sorry to hear that. But I'm worried about you. Where are you sleeping?"

"I've been showering and catching naps at Sadie's house. And I know my way around this hospital, honey. Everyone's been very accommodating. Don't forget, I've worked here for years."

"I know. But, Mama, I'm not far from Dallas right now, I can come. Give you some relief."

"No. Don't do that, honey. I'll be fine. You have enough going on. And, honestly, I'm just sitting here with her." Then almost as an afterthought, she asked, "What do you mean you're not far from Dallas?"

"I went to see a band play tonight. We might use them for our wedding. Katy recommended them and they're just outside the city limits."

"It's late, honey. Is Roger with you?"

"No, Mama. He's not with me."

"Then Katy?"

"No, she's sick. Poor thing caught a flu bug. I'm with…Cooper."

"Oh, good." The relief in her mama's voice grated on Lauren's nerves. Blind faith, that's what it was. In Cooper's ability to keep her safe. The moon and the stars were lining up in his favor and she fought the notion, waging a war inside her head.

"Maybe I should move into Roger's apartment in town," she said. "To be closer to you."

Cooper's head jerked in her direction and she turned away from his intense stare. "I mean, he's out of town for several more days and I'm sure… I don't think he'd mind."

"Don't you dare leave Stone Ridge. Not on my account." Her mother's voice had a stern tone she didn't often hear. "You have appointments at the ranch. I know you've got tables to rent and caterers coming to give you quotes and florists coming out to see the lake."

"Yeah, that's all true, Mama." She thought about it a few moments. It would be inconvenient to move into town, even temporarily. She'd told Roger, since their engagement was short, she wanted to spend the remainder of that time with her mother. And he'd seemed perfectly fine with that. "Okay, I guess you're right. It's just… I feel bad for Sadie and for you."

"I'll be fine. You just concentrate on what you have to do."

"Thanks, Mama."

"Tell her hello," Cooper urged.

"Cooper says hello to you, Mama."

"Give that man a hug for me, will you?"

"I, uh, sure Mama."

"Good night, sweetie."

She hung up the phone, dropped it into her purse and stared out the window. Now what? She had Cooper on the brain. His scent traveled over to her, subtle and arousing, and the memory of that kiss was never far from her mind. They were going to be alone. For days. Together.

And that was only if she made it through tonight.

Thankfully, Cooper didn't say a word on the rest of the drive home.

Once he pulled into the garage and shut down the lights, she gripped the door handle and got out of the SUV, her high-heeled boots rapidly tapping against the garage floor. The door to the house was locked and Cooper brushed by her to open it.

As she entered, everything inside was quiet but for the tick-tocking of a clock in the parlor. Timed lights were on there and in the dining room, covering the high ceilings in beautifully sculpted shadows. She bypassed those rooms and headed to the staircase, Cooper just steps behind her. She was so mixed up inside, she wanted to lash out, to break something. Nothing was right anymore. Nothing seemed logical. Nothing made any sense.

She took one step up and then faltered. She couldn't go on this way. She couldn't go to sleep and wake up in the morning pretending nothing had happened between them tonight. Or last night in the gym. Or the first time he'd kissed her, either.

So she turned to face him. The shadows made him look dangerous and rugged and breathlessly appealing. But she couldn't let that sway her.

"Why'd you do it, Cooper? Why'd you kiss me?"

He ran his hand down his jaw and looked her straight in the eyes.

"You want the truth?"

"Yes," she said, taking a big gulp of air. "I want honesty."

"I couldn't...*not*."

Her brain didn't process that because she was shocked. "That's not a reason."

His eyes widened in horror that she didn't believe him. "It's the only one I've got."

"What, that you find me so darn irresistible that you can't keep from kissing me?"

Cooper took a step forward, gazing deep into her eyes, searching her face for a moment. "Apparently."

"Well, stop it."

"Is this where you slap my face and tell me to snap out of it?"

His *Moonstruck* reference didn't make her smile. This was serious. Cooper was messing with her mind. "Don't joke about this."

"I'm… I'm just as confused as you are, Lauren."

"And why is that?"

"Because there're a dozen reasons that I shouldn't be having this conversation with you. Mostly because you're here under my protection and I—"

"Your protection?" She scrunched her face up. Wow, was he off base. "It isn't the 1800s, Cooper. I don't need protecting."

The way his gaze latched onto hers frightened her a bit. He wasn't kidding. Nor had he misspoken, if she read his expression correctly. What in hell was going on?

"Okay," he finally relented. "But why did you kiss me back? Have you asked yourself that question?"

"That's all I've been doing."

"And?"

She could only give him the truth, as she knew it. "It's because…well, I've had a crush on you."

There, she'd said it. She'd gotten her big secret off

her chest. And now may the big blue ocean drag her out to sea, swallow her up and rid her of mortification.

"I know that."

She blinked. Her heart raced even faster than when he'd kissed her. "You do? How?"

"A guy just knows. And, of course, Tony had a big mouth."

"My brother told you! I didn't think he knew, either."

"Doesn't matter now. What does a teen crush have to do with tonight?"

Oh, no. She squeezed her eyes closed briefly. "Don't make me say it."

He shook his head, appearing entirely clueless. "Say what?"

Where was that big, blue ocean when she needed it? "That my crush lasted a bit longer than that, Cooper. And when you kiss me, it's just an indulgence of mine, because…because I've imagined it for so long."

Cooper stood there, immobilized. There was a stark expression on his face. His mouth was tight, his eyes blinking rapidly. Finally he scratched his head so hard a lock of hair fell onto his forehead. "So you're saying you kissed me back because of some fantasy notion in your head?"

Gosh, kill me now. "I wouldn't exactly put it that way. But, yeah, let's just say I was curious."

"Maybe the first time could be chalked up to curiosity. But the way you kissed me tonight wasn't like a woman in love, about to be married to another man."

Tears rushed to her eyes. He was right, but it was all wrong and she wasn't going down that fickle road again. She couldn't be like her father. She couldn't leave one man for another time after time. She'd spent her entire teen years doing that very thing and it was time to stop. *Damn it*.

She summoned strength and lifted her chin. "It was curiosity, Cooper. It killed the cat, remember? Don't you see? It can't be anything else." She backed up onto the next step of the staircase and whispered, "It just can't be."

"Horseshit," he muttered. "We've been circling around this thing between us for days now."

"There's no *thing*, Cooper." There couldn't be, and she'd lectured herself a dozen times about this. She couldn't fall for the next best wonderful thing, even if Cooper Stone was that and so much more. She'd made a commitment to Roger and it had to stand. It had to be honored.

Nearly missing the next step in her retreat, she reached for the staircase railing behind her. At that moment, Cooper lurched forward, ready to catch her fall, but she backed far away from him.

"You're afraid of me," he said. It wasn't a question. "That tells me all I need to know."

Her heart pounded hard, a little voice singing sweetly in her ear, telling her not to listen to her brain, telling her to go with her heart. She didn't trust that voice. "You're wrong, Cooper. I'm not afraid of you. I'm afraid…of myself."

His dark blond brows rose, his face softening as his gaze locked onto hers.

She wanted to scream at the unfairness in all of this. "Please don't mess this up for me," she said softly.

Cooper's sigh echoed in the room. "I just want you to be honest with yourself."

"Why does it matter to you?"

"I care about you, Laurie Loo. If you love Roger, I won't stand in your way. Did you get a chance to talk to him today?"

It was none of his business. Really, it wasn't. "Yes."

"He called you?"

She nodded, and then because her mama hadn't raised a liar, she shook her head. "I called him." And found a woman in his hotel room. And Lauren was pretty certain he'd lied to her about that resort project.

But Cooper didn't need to know that. Cooper didn't need to know anything more than that she was engaged to be married very soon. And that's all there was to it. "I'm going up now."

"Go. I'll be down here, having a drink or three." He sent her a crooked smile. One that always charmed. And then he was gone.

"I don't know what I would have done without your help, Katy. All this wedding planning is overwhelming," Lauren said on a deep sigh. She appreciated her bestie spending her Sunday off here at the ranch, helping her decide on the caterer, ordering the chairs and tables, picking out the theme colors of sage green and pale pink. Tomorrow she had a florist and a photographer coming to see the wedding location.

How strange this all felt. It was as if she was living in two separate worlds right now. One where she was the devoted fiancée planning and anticipating her dream wedding, and the other where Cooper Stone was the star of her fantasies. She couldn't have it both ways.

She had to put what happened between her and Cooper aside and move forward with her wedding plans. Things were in motion and now it was too late to back out. Not that she wanted to. She wanted to marry Roger. She couldn't let a few kisses from Cooper tilt her world upside down. She felt guilty enough about those kisses. And her mind was set on getting married.

"Hey, no problem," Katy said, breaking into her thoughts. "It's fun. As long as I'm spending someone else's money, that is." Katy had a silly smile on her face. Thankfully her flu had only lasted one full day. Now she was as upbeat as ever. She sipped iced tea and glanced at all the papers strewed about the kitchen table. "Aren't you having fun, Lauren?"

"Uh…well, I suppose." Her hesitation was showing, and darn it, she didn't want Katy or anyone else to know she'd been having doubts. Her wedding day would be here before she knew it. "There's so much to do in such a short span of time."

"You know…you don't have to rush into this. If it's too much for you, you can always push the wedding date up."

"The invitations have already been sent." And there simply wasn't time for getting cold feet. She nibbled on her lower lip, her mind wandering to Cooper World. He was always halfway on her brain, invading her thoughts, troubling her, reminding her she was about to make a lifelong commitment. Shouldn't she be thinking of Roger during this time? Shouldn't she be anxious to become his wife?

She'd texted him twice today, asking him to call her. She needed to hear his voice. To be reassured and comforted by him. Up until now, he hadn't returned her texts or called.

Her fiancé was MIA.

Katy's arm came around her shoulder, warming her in a hug, something she really needed right now. "Hey, I can see something's bothering you. What's up? Wedding day jitters?"

A ridiculous tear emerged and slid down her face. She wiped it away with the back of her hand. "I'm not sure. This is silly. I'm an emotional wreck today. Sorry, Katy."

"Don't be sorry. I've heard lots of brides get like this before the wedding. And your wedding is on fast forward. I can see how all of this is making you a little emotional."

"Go figure, me being a bridezilla."

"You're not even close. Look how much you've already accomplished without much fuss at all."

"I guess so."

"Hey, you know what? We've been head deep in all this wedding stuff all day long. I think you need to let your creative juices flow on something else. Why not take advantage of this amazing kitchen and put your skills to use? You promised me you'd make me dinner here one night. Why not tonight?"

She wasn't in a creative mood at all. In fact, her

mood was becoming glummer by the second. She hadn't seen Cooper since last night and her head was spinning. Where was he? How awkward would it be when they saw each other again? Why couldn't she put him and that kiss out of her mind?

Yet she didn't have the heart to refuse Katy's request. Her friend had helped her so much today. Plus, they'd skipped lunch. Making dinner in this to-die-for kitchen might just perk her up. "What should I make?"

Katy put her elbows on the table and rested her chin on her fists. "Surprise me."

It appeared she had an audience of one. "Okay. I'll do my best."

An hour and a half later, the skirt steak marinated in oils and garlic sizzled on the countertop grill, and bacon-wrapped asparagus steamed in a quick-fry pan. Lauren's corn soufflé was just about ready to come out of the oven. After she put together the quinoa salad drizzled with balsamic vinegar, Lauren's masterpiece meal was almost done.

"My mouth is watering," Katy said as she set out the dinner plates.

"I hope my cooking doesn't disappoint," Lauren said.

"Something sure does smell good in here." The sound of Cooper's voice brought butterflies to her belly. She turned, finding him leaning up against the kitchen doorway, arms folded, one boot crossed over the other, nonchalant. How could he be so calm? So incredibly at ease, when she'd been confused, frustrated and full of self-doubt.

"Oh, hey, Cooper," Katy said. "Are you joining us for dinner?" She took out an extra plate from the cupboard. "Chef Lauren has been working magic in your kitchen."

Lauren remained quiet as Cooper's gaze focused on her. "Chef Lauren? That's a new one."

"She's been dying to get her hands on your, uh...appliances." Katy's gaze darted from Cooper to Lauren and she immediately clamped her mouth shut.

Oh, man. This was weird. "Of course you're welcome to join us, unless you have other plans tonight?"

"No other plans," he said, his eyes meeting hers solidly. "But are you sure?"

She blinked and nodded. She couldn't very well ace Cooper out of his own kitchen. "I'm sure."

"Thanks. I'd love to try one of your creations."

"Great," Katy said. "Lauren's going to have to share these recipes with me. My brother's birthday is coming up and Pete's the ultimate bachelor, a cop who solves crimes but doesn't know a spatula from a potato peeler."

Lauren chuckled. "I wouldn't go that far. Pete's a pretty smart guy."

"Still, I think he'd love a home-cooked meal for his birthday."

"Go for it." Lauren turned back to her cooking and Cooper came up behind her.

"Need some help?"

Her heart sped wildly. She needed to get a grip.

She spun around and crammed two pot holders into his hands. "Please take the soufflé out of the oven."

"Soufflé? Yeah, sure." He grinned at her and she made fast work of tending to the quinoa salad as he pulled out the dish and brought it to the island countertop.

A few minutes later they were all seated at the table, Katy chattering on and on about Cooper's cool kitchen and the wedding and anything else that popped into her head. Dear sweet Katy was the buffer Lauren needed between her and Cooper. And because of it, her nerves settled down as she glanced at Cooper, so strong, so incredibly sexy…yes, sexy. The guy couldn't help it. He was hunk material and she prayed that was all there was to her crazy infatuation.

Cooper made approving noises in his throat as he tasted the meal. "This is really good," he said.

"Thanks." She hadn't really said much to him at all tonight. "I love experimenting."

"So, did you always like cooking?" he asked as he forked up a piece of steak.

She nodded. It was a safe enough subject. "I was sort of forced into it. My mom worked long shifts at the hospital. So I'd play around with food, started following some cooking shows, and then got pretty decent at it. It was important for my mom to come home to a home-cooked meal already prepared for her. And it meant Tony didn't eat pizza and frozen dinners every night, too."

"You're amazing," Katy said. "Such a nurturer."

Cooper stared into Lauren's eyes and nodded. "The food's delicious. Katy's right. You are amazing."

Katy's eyes widened; Lauren's bestie clearly noticed there was something going on between them.

They finished the rest of the meal in silence and as soon as Katy scooped up her last bite, she rose. "Let me help with the dishes and then I'm out of here. I have to be at work early tomorrow."

"Don't be silly. You're not doing the dishes," Lauren said. "You've already done enough for me today."

Katy glanced at Cooper, who rose from his seat and began clearing off the table. "We've got this," he said. "But it was nice having dinner with you, Katy."

"Same here, Cooper. I'd better get going." She glanced at Lauren. "Walk me out?"

"Uh, sure."

Katy grabbed her hand and tugged her to the front door. "What on earth is going on between you two?" she whispered.

Lauren opened her mouth to deny any charges but then slammed her lips shut.

"There is something, isn't there?" Katy asked in a tone that required an answer.

Lauren nodded. "But I don't know where it's headed. And what to do about Roger."

"Are you saying you might be falling in love with Cooper?"

"I don't know. I don't know. What should I do?"

After Katy picked her jaw up off the floor, a look of sincere concern entered her eyes. "This isn't you being fickle, is it, honey?"

"I hate that word."

"I know, but this is serious. If you don't love Roger, or have any doubts, you need to break it off with him. You can't marry a man you're not sure about."

Lauren's shoulders slumped. "Oh, God. I know that. But what if it's just me being me. I mean, look at my father's history. Married and divorced four times. He couldn't choose. He was fickle."

"Your dad was a cheater. I'm sorry to say it so bluntly, but he was, and that's so not you. You're not like your father. You're a woman with a big, loving heart, and right now, if that heart isn't pointing you toward Roger, you need to recognize that. Soon."

"How soon?"

"As soon as you know."

Lauren let out a long-suffering sigh. "You're right. I have to figure all this out."

"You do that. And let me know if I can help in any way." Katy kissed her cheek. "I have faith in you. You'll work it out."

They hugged tight and then Katy was off.

Lauren took a steadying breath and walked back into the kitchen. Cooper stood by the sink with a dish towel on his shoulder, rinsing a dish. "Let me clean up," she said rather harshly and then softened her tone. "I mean, I made the mess. You must have something more important to do."

"Actually, I'm pretty free tonight." His eyes flickered over her body and a blast of heat rose up her neck. She was a mess, with flour smudges on her shirt and a grease stain on her jeans, her hair falling out of her tiny ponytail. "You go on. I can handle this."

Her sense of duty and her manners kicked in. She wasn't going to have Cooper clean the kitchen by himself. "No. You go on. I'll take care of this."

He didn't budge.

She walked over to the sink and nudged him away. Or tried to. Living up to his name, the man was made of stone. "Cooper." Exasperated, she reached for the soapy dish he held and the darn thing slipped, broke in two and sliced into Cooper's right hand. Blood spurted from his palm. Soon the entire sink was covered in it.

"Oh, no. I'm so sorry."

"It's okay," he said through clenched teeth.

It was so not okay. The pain must've been something fierce. She gripped his hand, quickly wrapped the dish towel around the cut and applied pressure. The towel soaked through and turned crimson immediately. She grabbed for another. "We've got to move. I need to stop this bleeding."

She held his arm upright and they strode out of the kitchen and up the stairs. She knew where the first-aid kit was stored: in his master bathroom.

She was such a fool for arguing with him. Such a fool for being stubborn. When would she learn? When would she see that fighting whatever this was between them was fruitless? It only caused more problems.

They made it into his bathroom quickly. "Lean against the counter." She pulled his arm over the sink and ran warm water over the cut. She cleansed it the best she could as blood continued to ooze out, but thankfully, not as profusely as before. "One second. Keep your hand still."

She grabbed the first-aid kit from the cabinet and took hold of his hand carefully. The wound was about half an inch long, not as bad as she'd initially thought. She applied antibiotic cream to his palm, gently working it in, and then wrapped a gauze bandage between his thumb and index finger, winding it around and around to immobilize his palm. Tying it off, she studied her work. "There," she said. "How's that?"

"The patient will live," he said.

"I'll have to rewrap it again soon. But hopefully most of the bleeding has stopped."

He nodded, glancing at his bandaged hand.

"I'm so sorry, Cooper," she said. "I'm such a jerk for arguing with you."

"You're not a jerk," he said quietly.

"I am."

"If you insist."

She snapped her head up and found his eyes twinkling. During the crisis, she'd been working next to him by the sink, but now, as he turned toward her, she found herself sandwiched between his legs. Her heart sped and her mind raced. The most worrisome thing was that nothing about this situation felt wrong.

"You're teasing me?" she asked.

"You know what they say about payback…it's a bitch."

"I don't tease you…"

"Just every second of every day you're under my roof." There was reluctance in his tone, but sincerity, too, and her bones were beginning a slow, steady meltdown. "You're smart and sweet and pretty and—"

She put two fingers to his lips. "Shush."

It was a mistake to touch his mouth, to witness the blue spark in his eyes. To see him struggle with desire as much as she was. He reached up with his good hand and held her fingers there. Then he kissed them, one at a time, slowly, his gaze touching her as candidly as his kisses.

"Cooper," she breathed, but a refusal died in her throat. It was the only thing dead inside her. Everything else bounced and jumped and marched through her body like a thirty-piece band.

"What?" he said, unfolding her hand and planting tiny, moist kisses there.

Strike up the band.

"This isn't—"

"It feels right, Lauren. Like it's meant to be. Tell me you haven't felt it, too."

"Too many times in my lifetime."

"That isn't what this is about," he said. "And you'd be lying to yourself to say it was."

Oh, God. It was true. It was different with Cooper. He wasn't only a crush. He was a friend, a man she admired, someone who would never hurt her. "I don't lie."

"Exactly," he said, taking her shirt into his fist and inching her forward a little bit at a time. When his gorgeous face lined up with hers, his lips came down hard, crushing and claiming and cradling her mouth in one generous kiss after another. Their hips met; her body, fluid and eager, meshed with his. This was no joke: the man was serious and every bit of his hard body was insisting she take notice. How could she not? How could she back away from a man she'd always secretly wanted?

She looped her arms around his neck and managed her engagement ring off her finger. She couldn't even think about Roger now, and what she would say to him. But the ring slipped off easily—it was never a good fit—and she palmed it into her pocket.

Did this make her un-engaged? In her heart, yes.

Cooper groaned and held her even tighter, his arms around her waist, pulling her closer. His arousal pressed against her, exciting her, making her whimper. Everything else around her dropped away. She was where she wanted and needed to be at the moment. With Cooper. It was like a freaking dream, one she'd had as a young girl, one she'd always wanted. But Cooper had always been forbidden, off-limits and, yeah, sort of an impossibility. Until now.

Their tongues touched, setting off an explosion in her body. Heat, passion and incredible want turned her inside out. Grabbing the material of his shirt, she pulled it apart—hallelujah for snap-down buttons—exposing his solid, rock-hard chest. Her fingers inched up his torso to palm the flat planes. His skin was hot, his heart pulsing under her fingertips.

"Coop," she whispered, pressing her lips to his chest. Kissing him, touching him, she was in Heaven.

He lifted her face from his chest, kissed her then moved her slightly away. "Fair play," he murmured. He began working the buttons of her shirt and soon the night air was cooling her flamed skin. In what seemed like one swift move, Cooper managed to get her shirt off and to drop her bra to the floor. Then his hot mouth resumed licking at her flesh.

He cupped one breast in his hand and suckled her, moistening her nipple. A shot of heat arrowed down her belly, traveled below her waist and landed at her core. "Ah-hh," she cried, her voice high.

Cooper was merciless as he continued to the other breast. When she didn't think she could stand it anymore, he lifted her into his arms, kissing her as he strode the distance to his massive king-size bed.

They were both bare from the waist up, and after he lowered her onto his bed, he came over her like a giant, gorgeous beast. "You want this?" he asked, desperately searching her eyes.

She gulped and nodded. "I want this," she whispered.

It was a formality. Because in Cooper's arms, she was toast. He had to know it, had to feel it as strongly as she did. She craved him from deep down and it wasn't only lust, but much, much more.

The corner of his mouth twitched up as he nodded. He rose from her and cradled her foot in his hands. One shoe dropped onto the floor then the other. "Lift your hips," he commanded.

She arched her back and he unzipped her jeans and tugged them down and off her legs.

His gaze landed on her teensy-tiny bikini panties and he smiled. The bright hungry gleam in his eyes encouraged her boldness. When she might've covered up, she simply laid there naked and allowed him to look at her.

After removing his boots, he climbed onto the bed, kissed her a dozen times and then moved down the edge of the mattress. He stroked her thighs, his caresses bold, demanding, and then he parted her legs. The scruffy whiskers on his face abraded the softest, most tender part of her body. And then her panties were gone and his mouth began an amazing torturous journey over her, inside her, kissing, stroking, his tongue gliding home.

She gripped the bedcovers and gritted her teeth. Moans of ecstasy poured out of her mouth. This was beyond heavenly. Beyond anything she'd ever experienced. He grasped her behind, lifting her slightly, and tasted her over and over, making incredibly erotic sounds with his throat. She'd never felt prettier, more desired. His fingers and mouth worked magic, and her cries echoed in the room as strong, hot waves built higher and higher inside her.

"Cooper," she called out as her final bit of restraint shattered in a moment of perfect release.

"I'm right with you, baby," he rasped.

Yes, he was. It was exactly where she wanted him to be as her sated body relaxed in the aftermath of her orgasm.

Cooper came up over her. "You are beautiful like this, but we're not done."

She smiled and curled her fingers into his hair. "I hope not," she said softly.

His deep ocean-blue gaze pierced her again, those

rays homing in, killing her with the depth of his emotion and desire. "You've destroyed all my willpower," he said.

She closed her eyes, smiling. "I feel the same way."

He kissed her tenderly, suckling her lower lip and murmuring, "Maybe it's time we gave up the battle."

"I surrender," she said, meaning it from the bottom of her heart.

"Laurie Loo, you have no idea…"

She roped her arms around his neck and brushed her lips against his, over and over. "I think I do."

A guttural groan escaped his throat and he worked like mad pulling his jeans off. His briefs came next and then he was naked, rising above her, his form solid, rock-hard. And, oh, man, was he well-endowed.

She touched him, her fingertips sliding over his shaft, and he jerked back, surprise and pleasure twisting his face. Cooper seemed to inspire audacious behavior and, for her, it was new, exciting and incredibly empowering. She wanted more, to taste him the way he'd tasted her, and as she lifted up to do that very thing Cooper shook his head, pulling away. "I want you that way," he murmured, "but it'll be the death of me right now, baby."

Hunger blazed in his eyes and a desperate plea for understanding. He didn't want to deny her anything, but he was just as blown away as she was. Emotions filled her up inside and she nodded to him, telling him she understood.

He opened his nightstand drawer and came up with a gold packet. A moment later, sheathed in a condom,

Cooper covered her mouth with his, his hands moving over the slope of her breasts and lingering there, caressing her to the point of unbelievable craving. Below her waist, her nerves pulsed, swamped with heat.

"Relax, Laurie Loo," he whispered, easing himself inside her.

Her body accommodated him, expanding to the length and width of him. Their joining brought tears to her eyes. But she wouldn't cry. Cooper couldn't get the wrong idea, that she was somehow sorry about any of this. Because, she was so *not* sorry. Being cradled in his arms, joined with him, his body slowly driving inside her, stroking her as he covered her in kiss after kiss, only brought joy to her heart.

This time, she hadn't made the wrong choice.

This time, she was in it for keeps.

All other men in her life faded away and only Cooper was there, filling her. Granting her freedom from her otherwise bad mistakes.

She moved with him now, her body a physical and emotional mate to his. She touched him everywhere, caressing his back and shoulders, gripped the firm slope of his ass, and, oh, man, he was strong, powerful. She tugged on his hair, kissed the scruff on his face and licked at his skin.

It was better than any dream she might've had of him.

He was real. And glorious.

And as his thrusts grew harder, she rose with him, higher and higher, until she couldn't hold on any longer. Her second release came fast and hard, and her cries rang out, sounding blissfully tortured.

"Lauren, baby," Cooper rasped in awe as he, too, reached his uttermost climax.

He ground out her name as he thrust into her one last fulfilling time.

And then silence surrounded them.

He fell on top of her, spent and heavy, his skin still deliciously steamy. She held him tight and they lay together that way for beautiful seconds. Those moments of realization becoming precious to her. Was it that way for him, too?

Finally, Cooper rolled off her and gathered her into his arms. His eyes sparkling, a charming smile on his face, he spoke quietly. "Wow. That was something."

She laughed, joy crowding her heart. "I'll say."

"Are you all right?" he asked.

"I'm wonderful."

He nodded, and gripped her tighter, drawing her even closer. The subtle musk of his aftershave mingling with the scent of his skin was like an aphrodisiac. As if she needed any more reason to find him so darn appealing.

"Yeah, me, too," he said, his voice trailing off.

"Don't you dare head into la-la land, Coop."

"Why, you have more plans for me?" A wicked, totally endearing smile spread across his face.

"Darn right, I do. I have to change your bandage before you fall asleep."

"Before *we* fall asleep, Nurse Abbott," he said, kissing the top of her head. "Got that?"

"Loud and clear."

Seven

Jogging beside Cooper the very next morning, a sense of freedom and exhilaration strummed through Lauren's veins. Since her time here, May had become June. The morning air was fresh and the sky gloriously blue, the rising sun casting a golden light onto Stone Ridge. This time, she kept up with him. Or rather, he slowed his pace to keep time with her as they cut a path away from the house, away from the stables and barns, running deep onto the property.

She noticed Cooper avoiding the lake and anything that would remind them about the wedding she had planned with another man. Honestly, she didn't know what was wrong with her. Normally, she'd be freaking out about this: the fact that she was so deeply in the moment with Cooper Stone while still formally engaged to her fiancé. She was going to remedy that as soon as Roger returned. She would break off her engagement in person. She owed him that much. It would be difficult, but Roger deserved to hear from her face-to-face.

Her head was finally clear and hopelessly wrapped around being with Cooper. So she ran on, with him at her side, a smile on her face and only good things in her heart.

Thirty minutes into the run, Cooper slowed his pace. "Ready for a water break?"

Sweat dripped from his forehead onto his T-shirt, his chest pumping hard, but it was clear he was stopping for her. They'd left cattle and grazing land far behind and she'd been struggling on the rocky uphill paths for a time now.

"I can go another few miles. But, sure, let's stop for as long as you need to."

He shook his head, mumbling something that sounded like brat, and led her to a patch of shade under an ancient tree. He was a good man. Always thinking about her, enough to slow his regular routine to make sure she was comfortable.

He'd sure given her a workout last night, a wondrous night she'd never forget. This morning she'd woken up beside him to watch the dawn light play over the rugged planes of his face. Blissfully happy, she'd curled her finger around a dark blond strand of his hair. When his eyes popped open, he'd smiled at her, and that one look had been enough to right her crazy upturned world. A few kisses later she'd been sure he was ready for round two, but he'd bounded out of bed and asked her to run with him.

They stood sipping from their water bottles, catching their breath. Early dawn had broken on this high ground, the land all around quiet and serene. Stone property stretched beneath them in all directions as far as the eye could see. From their perch atop this one hill, the ranch house looked miniscule.

Off in the distance birds chirped a cheery hello and soft breezes ruffled leaves on the trees. All in all, it was the perfect place to clear the mind.

She slipped her water bottle back into her belted bag.

"Wanna sit awhile?" Cooper asked.

She really did. "Sure."

She sat on a patch of grassy ground and Cooper sat behind her, spreading his legs out. "Lean back against me and get comfortable."

She did, and he wrapped his arms around her waist. He made a nice cushion, hard but accommodating. "This is nice."

"It is," he agreed, setting her ponytail to one side and kissing the slope of her neck.

"I'm all sweaty," she said, embarrassed.

"I like getting you sweaty. In all different ways."

She laughed at his nonsense. "Well, you surely gave me a workout this morning."

"Too much?" he asked.

"I'm holding my own."

"That's one of the things I really like about you. You don't complain or whine. You just get it done."

"Hardly. I'm not as decisive as I want to be."

Cooper sat up, closing in on her. His breath tickled her cheek and his voice lowered as he spoke into her ear. "Aren't we gonna talk about it, Laurie Loo?"

She squeezed her eyes closed. Thank goodness he couldn't see the pain on her face. "I don't want to." She didn't. It was messy and difficult and she wanted it all to disappear. Magically.

"You have to think about it sometime."

She touched the bare ring finger on her left hand. "I've already done something about it. In my heart."

Cooper didn't say anything. He sat stiff and motionless for what seemed like eons. It worried her. Was it too soon to speak about her heart's desire? Was he sorry they'd slipped last night? Now could they never go back to just being friends?

"Cooper, please say something."

"Okay. I will. Last night was the best night of my life."

Thank God. Her shoulders sagged in relief. She could finally admit to herself that it had been Cooper all along. He was the man for her. "Mine, too. I just need some...time to, uh, figure it all out."

Cooper dropped his hands away and she immediately missed him. "You want me to back off, give you time?"

She whirled around to face him. Sitting on her knees, she took his face into her hands. "No. Never. Cooper, I'm just asking for your patience... I've never done anything like this before in my life." Well, she had jumped from one man to another in the past. She'd just never slept with one man while dating and almost marrying another. "Tell me it's okay."

She kissed him and the explosion of fire and heat burned through her. The sparks that flew when they touched like this was proof positive that she was all-in with Cooper. She couldn't imagine herself with any-one else now.

But dealing with Roger and canceling the wedding made her stomach ache, so she backed away from the kiss. It was all too much, too soon.

"It's okay." Cooper sighed and rose from their lit-tle refuge. He offered his hand and she grabbed it and bounced up, too.

"Race you to the bottom of the hill," she said.

"You're on. I'll give you a head start."

"No way. I can hold my own."

"Just go, Laurie Loo. For once, don't argue."

That sounded like a good plan. She spun around and took off running as fast as she could, laughter rumbling from her belly and catching on the breeze. She ran long and hard, and from behind she heard the clop, clop, clop of Cooper's shoes pounding the earth. Just before she reached the bottom of the hill, he took the lead, his hand slapping her butt before he built up momentum and soared past her. Once he reached the bottom of the hill, he turned and waited for her.

"C'mon, slowpoke."

"Slowpoke, my ass."

He blinked and a wide smile graced his sweaty, gor-geous face. "I like it when you talk dirty."

She blew off that comment. It could get her in even more trouble. "Who knew you were so competitive."

"Guilty as charged. I don't take challenges lightly. I like to win and I don't apologize for it."

She thought about it a second. "I never knew that about you."

"I don't brag. I just get the job done."

Maybe she really didn't know the grown-up Cooper all that much. "I can see that."

"At least you're not a sore loser," he said, taking her into his arms. They were still far enough away from the house and any wandering eyes.

"I don't like losing, either. But I can handle it. Growing up without a dad around made me tough. There were no father/daughter dances for me, but I had my big brother when I really needed him."

"Yeah, and now you have me."

If only she knew what he meant by that. Did she have him? Or was this a fling? An affair to add a little spice in his life? Or worse yet, was she the guest of honor at Cooper's pity party for her?

Suddenly confused, she battled a surge of guilt about Roger, too.

Cooper's eyes softened and his rough, strong hands caressed her arms, stroking her with the gentlest touch. Her skin prickled and warmth spread up and down her body.

"Don't beat yourself up." It was as if he could read her mind. And then he bent his head and poured himself into giving her a mind-blowing kiss, one that took away her guilt, her remorse, her doubt. One kiss from Cooper could do all that.

"I'll try," she whispered.

"It's gonna be all right," he said, reassuring her. "Let's get going. I need a shower."

"I do, too."

Cooper's eyes danced as they touched upon hers. "I don't believe in wasting water."

Locked in his embrace, she couldn't focus on anything but him. And the charming, dastardly smile on his face. "You don't?"

"Nope. We all need to conserve…for the, uh, environment."

"The environment, huh?"

"Yeah, are you with me?" he rasped, touching his lips to hers again.

Her heart, pounding like hard rain, had yet to settle down. "Yeah, I'm with you, Coop," she whispered. How could she not be?

Water slashed over them, the pulsing shower washing off the sweat and heat of the run. Cooper lathered her up with a fragrant bar of soap. He turned her around and around, making sure every tiny part of her was well cleansed. "Feel good?" he asked.

"Hmm." He had no idea. Her eyes closed, she absorbed the rough yet gentle way he was washing her, his palms traveling the length of her body, over her shoulders, breasts, arms and legs. Then he spun her around and scrubbed her, sliding his soapy hands down the curve of her back and onto the slope of her ass. He spent a good deal of time there and a new heat began building in her body.

Reaching down, his fingers lightly touched her sensitive folds and she jumped.

"Hang on, baby," he said, kissing the back of her shoulders.

It was hard hanging on. Every touch was excruciatingly pleasant. And her mind was already twenty moves ahead, longing to join their bodies again. To feel the sensation of being one with Cooper. "When is it my turn?" she asked impatiently. She wanted her hands on him. To create the same sort of torture he was creating for her.

"Now would be a good time," he said, turning her around and handing her the soap.

The breath stuck in her throat when she saw his erection. It was hard to miss, and a crooked smile graced his face. "Clean me," he said.

She gulped and nodded, eager to touch him, to lay her palms on his body. She put her hands on his face first and kissed him. He growled from the depths of his throat and from then on it was a frenzy of palms on skin, touching, rubbing, caressing, the soap making it easy to glide and slide all over his massive body. She saved the best for last, making him wait, making him even harder.

Then she touched his shaft, her soapy hands wrapping around him and stroking up and down.

He clenched his teeth, gritting out words of encouragement. Empowered, she kept it up and, after a few more bold moves, he grabbed her wrists and stopped her. "Wait here."

A few seconds passed and when he returned, he was sheathed in a condom. The shower door closed behind him and water continued to rain down as he kissed her a dozen times and then she was lifted into his arms. On instinct her legs wrapped around his waist and he moved her to the stone wall of the shower. She was beyond turned on. She'd never made love this way before. It was so bold, so sensual.

Cooper nudged her with the tip of his shaft and as she opened for him, he impaled her with the full force of his erection. Their moans echoed against the tiled walls, competing with the pulsing thrum of the shower. She'd never felt so complete, so at peace, so totally willing to give herself up to this man.

His thrusts possessed her, claimed her, and the potent look in his eyes told her things that words alone could not say. She moved with him, giving him silent permission to take her to places she'd never been before. He pressed his tongue to her breast, licking the water off, kissing the very tip and creating white-hot heat that made her crazy.

She thrust against him now, her body arching up and then pressing down upon him, her arms clinging to his neck. "Ah, Lauren," he sighed.

In that moment, as her release was edging closer, she fell hopelessly in love with Cooper Stone. It wasn't about sex. It wasn't about lust or the fact that he was a rock-hard, gorgeous hunk. It was because she trusted him. With her heart.

"Coop," she cried.

"Babe," he growled through clamped teeth as he thrust one last time.

Seeing him shatter, seeing the intense look of pleasure on his face, was a beautiful thing.

And then she reached her climax—a tightening, final pulsing contraction that brought so much damn joy.

As they came down slowly, Cooper nuzzled her neck. "Oh, man."

"Wow," she said, still wrapped around his body, still joined to him.

"I like getting clean with you," he whispered.

"That's my line, Cooper," she said softly in the mellow afterglow of making love. "I've never been quite so *clean* before."

He chuckled as he turned off the spray and lowered her down, her feet hitting the pebble-tiled floor.

"Let's get dry," he said.

"Okay. I'd better go to my room. Just in case Marie comes in."

She pushed the shower door open and Cooper's hand came out around her waist, pulling her back inside. "Not so fast, Laurie Loo. Marie's not here. I gave her a few days off."

She blinked. "Seriously? You were so sure about this?"

Drops of water dripped off his broad shoulder as he shrugged. "Honey, I'm not sure of anything. But we need some privacy to figure it out." His mouth touched hers and he kissed her tenderly. "Unless you'd rather not be alone with me."

"I, uh, didn't say that." She curled her finger around a single strand of his dark blond hair. "I sorta like being with you. In case you haven't noticed."

"I was hoping."

Gosh, he made it easy for her to be with him. He was so damned understanding. What was she going to do if this turned out to only be a brief interlude? Cooper hadn't said anything about the future, but maybe it was too soon. He was considerate enough not to overwhelm her. She still wasn't free of Roger. She had to believe that whatever Cooper was feeling for her mirrored her own intense feelings.

No matter what happened between her and Coop, she was done with Roger. And he deserved to know the truth. She needed to break it off with him to his face. She needed to find the right words, to look into his eyes and tell him that she wasn't in love with him. Not the world-tilting, earth-shattering, heart-melting way she should be. She cared about him and respected him and only a face-to-face breakup would do.

Cooper opened the shower door and allowed her to step out first. She grabbed a fluffy white towel and he instantly took it out of her hands. "Let me."

"Okay, but as soon as you're through, I need to bandage you up again."

"It doesn't hurt anymore." He showed her his palm and she cringed when she saw the red gash. "I think touching you has healed me."

"If only."

"It could happen. You're soft and sleek and silky smooth. Especially when you're wet."

He used the towel to dab at her naked body, sopping up droplets on her breasts and belly and lower still, coming dangerously close to arousing her again. She struggled, distracted, the words jumbling in her head. "I do, uh, need to bandage you up, Cooper."

"Yes, Nurse Abbott."

At least he agreed and there'd be no argument. She'd injured him with her little act of rebellion yesterday and still felt bad about it.

He continued to dab beads of water off her shoulders and back, then wound the towel around her backside. As he slid it back and forth, his hands *accidentally* slipped off the towel onto her butt cheeks. He gave her a little squeeze. *Wow.* Her juices started flowing again. She should have been flaming red by now, but with Cooper, it didn't feel off or weird. It felt sexy as sin. And in another minute, she'd be pushing him onto his massive king-size bed.

When he was done, she wrapped herself in the towel and faced him. "My turn."

He frowned as she grabbed another towel and made fast work of drying him off. Then she wound the towel around his waist and tucked it in, to give herself a sliver of sanity. But in or out of his towel, Cooper was irresistible.

She found the first aid-kit easily. "You know, for a house this size, you should have a few more of these around."

"What makes you think I don't?" he answered, smiling.

"Oh." Surprised, she asked, "So where are they?"

"Pretty much in every bathroom on the premises."

She blinked. "But you…you…led me to believe you—"

He kept his lips clamped shut, but laughter burst from his mouth anyway.

"You rat. You deceived me."

"I couldn't help it," he rasped. "I wasn't thinking straight last night. I mean all that blood loss made my mind fuzzy."

She slanted him a look and grabbed his injured hand.

"Ouch! Nurse Abbott, your bedside manner needs—"

She raised her eyebrows as she anticipated his next words.

"No improvement," he whispered from deep in his throat. "In fact, I'd say your bedside manner is outstanding in every way."

She sighed. "Cooper, what am I going to do with you?"

"You really don't want me to answer that, do you?" His gaze traveled toward his bedroom.

"No, don't answer."

"Too bad."

Cooper flipped flapjacks on the griddle as bacon sizzled and steam rose up in the pan. It'd been so long since he'd cooked anything in this kitchen, much less breakfast. On the days Marie wasn't there, he usually ate cold cereal or buttered a couple of slices of toast. This morning, he was cooking for Lauren. It surprised him how much she was on his mind lately. It came as a shock, a jolt from out of the blue, that he could ever have been so doggone attracted to her. But hormones and lust didn't give a fig about propriety. When the two of them were together, their chemistry was combustible.

But now that he'd slept with her, he'd have to face some hard facts. He'd broken a long-standing code of honor: you don't mess with your best friend's little sis. Not even if you're trying to protect her. Not even if she was about to make the mistake of her life.

But they had slept together and now the dawning consequences were closing in on him. Would she ever believe that sleeping with her had nothing to do with his determination to expose Roger and make her see the light? Would he ever be able to convince Lauren that he wasn't seducing her to break up her engagement? Would she believe he had started out only wanting to keep her out of harm's way but his feelings for her had surprised him and complicated matters?

Crap. He was in deep.

But not enough to give her up.

Not enough to own up to the little scheme he'd concocted with Loretta.

"Whoops. Something's ten seconds away from burning." Lauren's sweet voice did things to him. A sense of joy and *dread* stampeded through his body as she rushed across the kitchen and up to the stovetop. She shut down the bacon and removed the pan from the heat.

"I like it crispy," she said, chuckling.

"I knew that." No, he didn't. His mind had drifted off and he'd become derelict in his master chef duties, thinking about Lauren. "I aim to please, ma'am." He flipped the last of the flapjacks.

Her arms came around his waist from behind and she pressed up against him. She gave him a little peck of a kiss on his throat. She was killing him. When he was with her, all deceit and scheming faded from his mind and flashes of a future with her entered his head. Flashes that were becoming brighter, clearer, more distinct. But it was too soon to say anything. Too soon to act on his feelings because, if he was wrong, Lauren would get doubly hurt. And he couldn't have that.

He hadn't planned on breaking up her engagement this way. And how could he be sure his six-month long bout of celibacy hadn't influenced what he was feeling now? Was he falling for Lauren or had he just been overwhelmed by having a sexy, beautiful, forbidden woman under his roof every day?

No. Strike that.

The feelings he had for Lauren weren't just about lust.

He turned in her arms and kissed her full lips. "Breakfast is ready. Why don't you pour the coffee?"

Her face fell slightly, a hint of disappointment in her eyes. Hell, he wanted to kiss her senseless, but guilt was gnawing at him.

Lauren brought coffee mugs to the table and then set out maple syrup and butter while he dished out pancakes and the thick, almost-burned bacon to their plates. He noticed that lately she wasn't wearing her engagement ring. It was a sign, but she hadn't said anything to him about it.

They chowed down on the meal, speaking very little. Lauren's expression was unreadable, which was weird because she usually wore her heart on her sleeve. Right now, he had no clue what she was thinking.

He dove right in. "Have you spoken with Roger lately?" he asked quietly.

She put her head down and chewed her food thoughtfully. "Not since Saturday night. It was late and his secretary answered the phone."

"His secretary, huh? They were working in the office that late?"

"No, they were in the hotel room."

Cooper sighed. "So tell me, his secretary is gray at the temples and has been with him for years."

Lauren rolled her eyes.

"No?"

"Not even close. She's divorced and younger than me."

Cooper ran his hand through his hair, scratching at his scalp. "So...you haven't—"

"No, I haven't said anything to him. I figure I owe him an explanation face-to-face when he returns."

Which was in two days.

Cooper needed to say something to her. To make her feel better. To give her something she could hold on to. But the words wouldn't come.

His house phone rang and he stood to pick it up. "Hello?"

"Hello, Cooper. It's Loretta. How are you this morning?"

"Doing well. Just had some ridiculously good pancakes with your daughter. She's right here. Would you like to speak to her?"

"Yes, thank you."

He stared at Lauren and saw the misery on her face. Just a little while ago, she was beaming. All this talk about Roger Kelsey was getting to her. "Here you go."

He handed her the phone and began clearing the dishes. "Hi, Mama," he heard her say. "How's Sadie doing?"

Cooper left the room then to give her privacy. He walked into his study, plunked down on his big, cushy, leather chair and started going over accounts and purchase orders. There was a time when he could dig deep into the Stone Corporation and not come up for hours. Today wasn't one of those times. His mind was shot and the lack of concentration had everything to do with Lauren.

He ran a hand down his face.

And then heard her scream.

He dashed out of his study and ran toward the noise. His heart racing, he yanked open the front door and smacked right into Lauren's chest as she dashed into the house. Her eyes glazed over freakishly. He grasped her arms and steadied her. "What is it? What the hell scared you?"

"It's… I'm sorry. I'm usually not such a baby, but I was standing on the veranda drinking the last of my coffee and this…this *thing* scurried past me. I think it ran over my toes." She shivered. "Yuck. It was the ugliest creature I've ever seen."

"A possum?"

She nodded her head. "I mean, I've seen them on the road."

"Roadkill."

"Yeah, but I've never been that close up to one before. I think my scream woke the dead. Gosh, I'm so sorry."

"Don't be sorry. Sometimes my crew needs a good wake-up call," he said, cradling her shoulders and shutting the front door. He walked her into the large, formal, living room. Normally, he didn't set foot in there unless he was entertaining guests. It had been a good long time since he'd thrown a party. But the room was open and light, with tall ceilings and sitting areas where Lauren could calm her nerves. He led her to a sofa seat facing a large window that looked out on the pasture. The blue sky filled with white puffy clouds seemed almost touchable.

"This is silly. I'm an ER nurse for heaven's sake. I've seen a lot of horrible things."

"But you've never had an ugly-as-sin possum stalk you before."

She chuckled and her shoulders relaxed. "No, that much is true."

"How's your mama doing?" he asked. Changing the subject would help her, but it'd calm him down, too. After hearing her scream, he'd panicked and couldn't get to her fast enough. That alone unsettled him.

"She's doing well. Sadie is coming around. In fact, she's on the mend now and Mama's arranged for her to have assistance when she goes home. Should be in a day or two."

"That's a relief. Your mama is a good woman."

"The best. So, I guess she'll be coming back here soon." She put her head down and stared at her fingernails. How had life gotten so complicated? "Unless the painters are through with their work early and we can both move back into our house."

Cooper heard the pain in her voice. She was struggling with confronting Roger and what to do about Loretta. His hands were tied. It wasn't as if he could tell Lauren's mother that they'd been intimate. Cooper winced. He didn't have any answers, but one thing was certain: he didn't want to give up on Lauren. He didn't think he could.

"Hey, I have an idea," he said. Anything to perk her up and make her smile again. Anything to keep her near. "Do you trust me?"

She lifted her lids and tiny emerald flecks brightened in her eyes. She nodded.

"Good. Meet me outside in half an hour. Oh, and wear something…" He studied her appearance. Her hair was down, touching her shoulders. She wore a white midriff top exposing a slender slice of skin and a pair of skintight jeans that perfectly showcased her legs and ass. "Never mind, you're perfect the way you are."

It was true. Lauren was the closest thing to perfection he'd ever seen in a woman.

"Give me a hint?"

"No. But be sure to wear your riding boots."

"Riding boots? I don't have—"

"Okay, whatever you call those things you wear."

"My Steve Maddens?"

He shrugged. "Boots are boots. Wear them. And bring a jacket. I'll see you in half an hour."

He left her standing there, looking dumbfounded.

So was he. Because he'd never taken another soul to this very private place.

Eight

Lauren was mystified. She had no clue where Cooper was taking her but she'd packed her hobo handbag with essentials: lotion, keys, phone, tissues, hairbrush, antacid and a toothbrush. Yeah, a toothbrush. A girl had to keep up her dental health, didn't she?

She took a minute to steady her nerves. Heck, she had just about one hundred people invited to a wedding that would never be, and instead of facing facts and doing something about it, she was running off with Cooper. To who knew where.

Goose bumps broke out on her arms. Being with Cooper did that to her, but she couldn't deny it was wrong. Instead of being responsible and flying up to Houston to face Roger, she was going on an excursion of some sort with her brother's best friend.

And worse yet, she was thrilled at the prospect of more time with him.

She felt wicked and selfish and…glorious.

What a mess she'd gotten herself into.

One final look at herself in the mirror contradicted Cooper's claim that she was perfect. She was far from it, but his compliment did sink down into her heart and her wicked self glowed inside. On a sigh, she scooped up her bag, grabbed her hooded jacket and walked out of her bedroom.

At the base of the stairs, she scoped out the house. Cooper was nowhere in sight, so she took a peek outside, making sure no pesky varmints were about. Her toes curled at the thought of that giant animal still being around.

When she determined the coast was clear, she took one tentative step onto the veranda and then another. She spotted Cooper, riding a golden stallion. He had an equally beautiful steed in tow behind him. The horses were packed down with supplies.

Smooth as a cowboy from an old Western flick, Cooper dismounted and tipped his hat. "Ready for a ride?"

She gulped and stumbled back. "Don't you have work to do?"

"Not at the moment." He shrugged and a cocky smile spread across his face. "The advantages of being the half owner of Stone Corporation. My brother's in charge today."

"Nice of him."

Cooper pursed his lips. "Chicken?"

"Of...of what? No...of course not." She hadn't been on a horse since she was ten years old. But she'd sure treated a lot of wannabe cowboys in the ER who'd been trampled, stomped on and tossed off their feisty mounts. "I'm sort of partial to the Jeep. Can't we take that?"

"Not where we're going. It's better to travel on horseback."

Where on earth were they going?

He walked over to her. "C'mon," he said, taking her hand. "I won't let anything happen to you. This here is Daisy. She's a gentle mare and she needs the exercise."

Didn't he have ranch hands for that?

"She's pretty."

"Got the same honey tones as your hair."

"Uh-huh."

"Come say hello to her."

Cooper took her hand and placed it on the horse's flank. The horse didn't move, but Lauren sensed she liked the attention. She kept on stroking her. "Hello there, Daisy. Who's your friend?"

"This is Duke."

"Are they a couple?"

Cooper smiled. "More like father and daughter. Daisy's a two-year-old palomino born here on Stone Ridge."

The warmth and pride in Cooper's tone eased her nerves. "Oh, a family affair." She was touched that papa and filly were raised together on the ranch. "Where's Daisy's mama?"

"Duchess is in the corral. She's a bit older than Duke and needs to rest up."

Cooper stroked Duke's nose and fussed with his beautiful mane, untangling a few strands. Then he turned to face her. "Ready?"

She nodded. "As much as I'm gonna be."

"Left boot in the stirrup and then hoist on up," he said. She did so and only managed to get halfway up before Cooper's flat palm landed on her butt and gave her the boost she needed. His touch seared through her jeans and robbed her of breath.

"Good girl," he said. Was he speaking to the mare or to her? "Now, straddle the saddle, putting most of your weight in the center. That's it."

Once she was seated on the saddle, she looked at the ground and swallowed hard. It was a long way down. When she looked up again, she squinted into the late-morning sun.

"Hang on," Coop said, reaching for a tan felt hat that was at least a size too big for her. "Put this on."

She did and he nodded. "Cute."

"Cute? I can hardly see."

Cooper tipped the hat back a little on her head. "There," he said. "Better?"

She nodded, feeling like a child being shown how to put on her shoes. "Much."

"All right then." He handed her the reins, giving her basic instructions on how to manage the animal between her legs. "Remember subtle movements are best."

"Gotcha."

"Don't worry. Daisy will follow her papa. She won't stray. You just keep yourself centered in the saddle and there won't be a problem. Ready?"

"Ready."

Cooper mounted his horse efficiently and settled his butt into the saddle. He whistled, gave the horse a gentle tap with his heels, and Duke took off at a slow enough pace for Daisy to follow easily. Within minutes, the house and stables had vanished. They were headed south over terrain that didn't appear well traveled.

It was a seventy-five-degree day with breezes that sometimes required her to put a hand to her hat. The pastures were thick here, and few cattle roamed on this part of the land. "How many acres is Stone Ridge?" she asked.

"Twelve thousand."

"I didn't realize it was so big. Do you enjoy your work, Cooper?"

"I do. Not too many people can work from home and manage a corporation. I feel fortunate. I love the land here. Never wanted to do much else."

"Does Jared feel the same way?"

"Jared? I think he likes working the land. He's got other investments as well. But Stone Ridge has surely afforded him a way to indulge in his hobby."

"Which is?"

"Jared has a need for speed. In his off hours he's either racing his boat or riding his Harley. He's got quite a collection of sports cars too. He's an adrenaline junkie. Kinda worries me at times being he's my kid brother and all."

"I get that. It's a dangerous kind of hobby."

"Yep. But he's a smart guy and great partner, and never shirks his duties here. As far as ranching goes, I'm more hands-on."

"Tell me about it." *Whoops.* The comment had slipped out of her mouth.

His laughter boomed. "I didn't hear too many complaints last night or in the shower this morning."

She was tired of talking to the back of his head. She made a clucking noise and Daisy caught up to Duke so they were side to side. Cooper turned to face her. God, the man oozed masculinity in a cowboy, bad-ass way that stunned her sometimes. The black hat, the jeans, the muscular arms and the command he had of the animal tossed her crazy world on end. "I'm not complaining."

"Glad to hear it. Because if I have anything to say about it, these hands are gonna continue to keep real busy."

Memories of the magic his hands had already done made her dizzy. Cooper could turn her on with one simple innuendo. "Is that so?"

"It is so."

"I should be on a plane right now, heading to Roger. To explain."

"Roger Kelsey doesn't deserve you."

The implication was that Cooper did.

She let out a deep sigh and her shoulders sagged. But with a burst of courage, she asked the burning question. "What are we doing, Cooper?"

Without hesitation he answered, "We're not rushing

into anything. We're spending time together, grieving for your brother. We're helping each other and maybe helping ourselves at the same time."

She appreciated his candor. He didn't mince words. And put that way, it all made sense.

She nodded and took the bumps as her horse continued over the rough terrain.

She hoped this adventure with Cooper was worth the bruises her sore butt endured.

"Keep your eyes closed, Laurie Loo. We're almost there."

Good thing, because she was dusty, sweaty, and she could already feel her body rebelling like a son of a gun. "They're closed."

After another minute she heard leather cracking and sensed Cooper had dismounted and stood very close. "Okay."

"Okay?" She opened her eyes and faced a rustic structure made of wood and stone, set in a clearing surrounded by freshly planted trees. "What am I looking at?"

Cooper lifted his arms and helped her off Daisy. They stood facing each other. She wanted to wrap her arms around his neck and crush her mouth to his. After all, she'd done everything he'd asked without a single complaint. And she wanted a reward. But the pride in Cooper's eyes spoke of something more important.

"It's my cabin. And I haven't told a soul about it, except for my brother."

"A secret hideaway?"

"The fort wasn't big enough."

She stared at him. "Are you saying you built this by yourself?"

His head bobbed up and down. "I did. I've been working on it for the past six months."

"Since Tony's death. Why, Coop? I don't understand?"

"I needed a place to grieve. Someplace quiet, someplace where I could come to grips with my guilt. Someplace that would mean something one day. I put that energy into building this place. With my own hands. My father always said we wouldn't know a happy day until we built something from the ground up. So on the weekends and days when I wasn't needed on the ranch, I'd work here."

"Wow. This is amazing." She was impressed. There was more to Cooper Stone than good looks and great wealth. She'd always known that, but seeing what he'd accomplished put everything in perspective.

"I plan to make this place a horse rescue one day. For horses like Duchess, who are old and weary. They can live out their days in peace here. And I'm naming it after Tony. It'll be Double A Rescue."

"For Anthony Abbott," she said softly, her throat closing up and tears stinging her eyes. "I'm…honored that you brought me here."

"Like I said, we're helping each other…maybe?"

"Yes, I… I think we are." The tears spilled down her cheeks. She didn't have enough willpower to stop the flow. She'd never known a better man than Cooper Stone.

"Ah, baby," he said, kissing her teary cheeks. "Don't cry. That's not what this place is about."

"No, no. You're right. It's about hope and the future."

He wiped her eyes using the pads of his thumbs.

"Yeah, that's how I see it, too." He wrapped an arm around her shoulders. "C'mon. I want you to see the inside."

Shoulder-to-shoulder, they stepped up onto the porch. He shoved the door open and they entered. Sure, it was rustic, with wood beams and a brick fireplace, but it was also warm and cozy, a place where a caretaker to supervise the rescued horses might dwell one day. There were three big bedrooms. One housed a bed already, and she assumed Cooper used it on his weekends here. The kitchen was generous in size. No appliances were installed yet, but there was a refrigerator Coop told her worked on a generator. And, thankfully, the bathrooms had plumbing.

She could envision it all fully equipped and furnished. The cabin had Cooper's mark on it, unpolished around the edges but oh, so genuine and friendly. "I love this place." The awe in her voice couldn't be controlled. This was not only Cooper's place, it was Tony's.

That made it all the more special.

"I'm glad you like it."

"It's a labor of love, Coop," she said, touching his arm. "And I am very grateful you shared this with me."

Cooper looked down at the hand on his upper arm and sucked in a breath. The contact between them sizzled and she saw him battle for control. "I'm hungry. You?"

She blinked and nodded, a little bit disappointed. She was getting hot and cold signals from him. He said all the right things, but at times she felt him retreat, both mentally and physically. The doubt it left her with made her tummy ache.

Or was it only her imagination? Was she so darn consumed with him that she overthought every moment?

"Good. I packed enough food for a battalion. I'll bring it in."

"Need some help?" she called after him. He was already at the door.

"Nope. You just look around some more. I'll only be a minute."

She did just that. She moseyed around the three-bedroom cabin and looked out the kitchen window that faced a picturesque oak tree. There was a tire swing hanging from a thick branch. She could see Cooper on that thing, or leaning up against the base of the tree, taking a rest after a hard morning of work. It still amazed her that he'd built this cabin. The warmth flowing in her heart was laden with so much love, she could barely stand it.

"Here we go," Cooper said, coming inside loaded down with the supplies Daisy and Duke had carried on their backs.

"Set this out, would you?" he asked, handing her a blue-plaid blanket.

"Where?" The place was empty but for a few pieces of furniture.

"In the dining room, silly girl," Cooper said with a quirky smile on his face.

She smiled back. "Oh, right. I should've known."

Just outside the kitchen area was a room meant for dining. It wasn't overly large, but it surely could hold a table for six easily. She bent on her knees and spread out the blanket. Cooper handed her two plastic plates, a loaf of bread and two different kinds of chunk cheese. He opened a bottle of white wine and she held plastic cups as he poured.

There were cold cuts and peanut butter-and-jelly sandwiches, fresh fruit, along with three types of desserts. It was as if Cooper had a magic bag; he kept putting food out onto the blanket. Well, there was *something* magical about him. So magical that she was there with him carrying on an affair. Who knew when or how it would end, and still she wasn't balking. Still, she couldn't say no.

She was gloriously happy being there with him. Seeing how he'd poured his heart into every plank, every beam, every brick in this little hideaway quelled all of her doubts. When she was with Cooper, she felt closer to her brother. They both knew different sides of Tony, both cared about him beyond words, and yet when she and Cooper were together, it felt like the love they had for Tony was complete.

In a strange sort of way.

"What'll it be, Miss Quiet Over There?" Cooper asked.

She settled into a cross-legged position opposite him. "I'll have bread and a slice of that Gruyère."

He used a plastic knife to slice a piece of cheese then broke off a hunk of bread and plopped it onto her plate. "Here you go. Cuisine à la Texas."

She laughed and watched as he picked up a peanut butter-and-jelly sandwich and gobbled down a big bite. "Hmm. Goes good with wine," he said. He lifted his plastic cup.

She lifted hers, too, and they bumped cups.

"To Tony, to Double A Rescue and to Tony's little sister, Laurie Loo."

Cooper's eyes softened on her and his face lit up with something she dared not hope for. It was all she could do to keep her eyes dry and not fall into his arms. She inhaled. "And to Coop, Tony's bestie and a man who is good and honest and honorable. A man I'm proud to—"

But her words were muted as Cooper leaned over and brushed his lips to hers. The tenderness in his kiss startled her in a good way, melting her like a marshmallow over a campfire. She was in deep with Cooper and loved every second she spent with him.

"I don't deserve your praise," he whispered.

"Of course you do," she said, suddenly indignant on his behalf. "You're—"

He silenced her again, this time with two fingers to her lips. "Shush, Lauren. Please."

He leaned back and finished his sandwich, pretty much ending the toast and the conversation about his good qualities. He was humble and didn't want to hear compliments about his nature. And he was probably still feeling guilty about the way Tony had died. If only she could take Cooper's pain away and assure him he wasn't to blame. He was experiencing survivor guilt and she understood that. But not on her watch. She wasn't going to stand by and let him beat himself up day after day.

The conversation turned to the rescue and his plans for building a shelter and corrals for the animals. The land was wide open. He had acres that weren't suited for cattle he planned to put to good use for old, injured and abused animals.

She heard the excitement in his voice, the boyish enthusiasm he had for this project. She'd often been labeled a nurturer, which went with the territory of being a nurse. But shock of all shocks, she just realized that he was a nurturer, too. He hid it better than anyone she'd known, but it was there, once the layers were peeled away, just waiting to be discovered.

"I hope to open it up to students in the community. There are high school kids in the city who'd love to volunteer their time and learn how to care for animals in need."

"I would've jumped at the chance to come out here. I think it's a great plan."

"It's a beginning, anyway."

"You didn't want your crew or your friends to know about this?"

"No, I didn't." He poured another glass of wine for both of them. They weren't the big red cups, but smaller, so she had no qualms about accepting more wine. "I needed the solace, still do, to finish the place.

I don't want to answer questions about it or have to explain myself."

"It's a wonder no one's discovered it before."

"If they have, they haven't spoken of it to me. And that's just fine. It's pretty remote out here. Well away from the pasture and set back a bit."

"Tell me about the tire swing?"

He laughed. "You saw that?"

"I did. What's funny? I love it."

"It's just that I was watching an old movie one day not too long ago and saw a young boy riding on one in his backyard. His kid sister came by and pushed him off it and then took off running. He chased her but never did catch up. Reminded me of something you would've done with Tony. I don't know, there was something simple about it that called to me. And that giant oak out there was just begging for attention."

"Tony never could catch me." Images of her younger self horsing around with her brother flashed through her mind.

"That's not the way I heard it."

"It's a fact. Tony would *never* deliberately let me get away. He was too competitive for that. If I got away, which I did plenty of times, it was because I was faster than him."

Cooper shrugged. "Okay, I stand corrected. You're right about Tone. He was as competitive as I was. We both never backed down from a challenge. And we'd both thrash our bodies and back to rack up the win."

"Yeah, I remember Mama patching him up. Didn't

matter if it was football, track or gymnastics, he'd come home banged up."

"It was no different with me," Cooper said.

After she finished her bread and cheese, she unwrapped a kitchen towel filled with cookies, brownies and muffins. "What'll it be?" she asked him.

"I'll have one of each," he said.

She smiled. "Of course you will."

She nibbled on a chocolate-chip cookie while Cooper devoured a brownie. He poured another cup of wine. "Want one?"

"Sure, to wash down the cookie," she said, and he filled her cup. "I think I like picnicking indoors."

"Me, too," he said, polishing off the blueberry muffin.

"Tell me, Coop, how on earth do you stay so rock-hard?"

He sputtered wine and drops drizzled down his chin. Wiping it with the back of his hand, he answered right away. "Pretty much if I'm in the same room with you, I can't seem to help myself."

Instantly her face flamed and she covered her mouth with her hand. "Did I just ask you that?"

He scratched his head and grinned. "You sure did."

"I didn't mean it that way." But his answer sure was revealing.

Cooper scooted over to the wall and leaned against it. He crooked his finger, beckoning her to join him. Of course she went, because denying Cooper anything today wasn't happening. He opened his arms. She fit her body in his embrace and turned around, so her back was to his front. He wrapped his strong arms around her waist. "Lean back," he said.

He wanted to hold her and she wanted to be held. With her head under his chin, resting on his broad chest, she relaxed and snuggled in.

A sweet sigh blew from his mouth and warmed her ear. It was amazing that they could both be so calm when the pressure of his arousal was right there teasing her butt. But Cooper didn't move a muscle, except to ease his head back against the wall. And they sat there like that, speaking softly about the ranch, her work at the hospital, the latest blockbuster movie playing in town. Anything and everything, except the one thing that needed their attention.

Where they stood with each other.

Once she confronted Roger, then what?

Cooper had never mentioned anything about the future to her. He wanted her in the present, and maybe that was all she should dwell on. She was jumping too fast, leapfrogging from one situation to another. But would her heart be intact after she left Stone Ridge? Once she went back to her normal routine, if that were even possible now, would this thing with Cooper become a heartbreaking memory? *Oh, God.* She couldn't imagine life without Cooper in it. The emptiness inside would swallow her up and cause a giant divide, a space that no one else could fill. How could she have fallen so hard, so fast?

Because Cooper Stone was like no other man she'd ever met.

He must've caught her negative vibes and the stiffness taking over her shoulders. "Hey, remember the time you colored your hair purple?" he asked, brushing a kiss to her hair. The smile in his voice lifted her spirits.

"How could I forget? It was during my rebellious goth stage."

"Yeah, I remember. You looked—"

"Watch it, Stone." She could easily jab him in the ribs with her elbow.

He laughed and the vibration rumbled in his stomach and bounced her up and down a little. "Can't help recalling how pissed Tony was. He said you looked like a damn troll."

"Yeah, I got teased a lot in school and Mama had a hissy fit."

"Just goes to show, you can't change perfection, Laurie Loo."

She snorted. "I'm hardly perfect." But her ego, which had been dipping low, skyrocketed at his compliment.

"If you ask me, you are."

His flattery was killing her. "You know how my mother punished me for that act of rebellion?"

He shook his head. "I forget."

"She told me I couldn't color it back to my original blond, so I had to live with it until it faded or grew out. She said in life, you have to live with the decisions you make."

"So, it was a lesson."

"Yeah, big time."

"Was the lesson learned?"

She shrugged. "Maybe." At least in her professional life it was. Her private life was a different story. "But I still think it's important to act on your impulses once in a while, so you don't grow to regret what you missed out on in life. As painful as growing my hair out was, I think I would've still dyed it for the experience."

Cooper stroked her arm up and down, creating warm tingles inside her very relaxed body. Fatigue set in quickly and she struggled to keep her eyes open. The wine, the food, the soreness from the ride, all contributed to her bones going limp.

"What else have you done to warrant a lesson?" he asked.

She allowed her eyes to close now and snuggled deeper into Cooper's chest. "You," she whispered and then promptly fell asleep.

She was dreaming pleasantly just as a school bell began to ring and ring and ring. Her eyes popped open to Cooper's sharp profile. As she nestled in his arms on the floor, it all came back to her. That wasn't a school bell ringing, it was her cell phone!

Cooper woke, startled, and clutched her tighter to his body, but she disentangled herself from his arms. "Sorry, I have to get this. It could be my mother."

Crawling on the ground, she rummaged through her bag and found her phone. "It's from the hospital," she told him.

She had a very brief conversation and then hung up.

Cooper was still coming out of his nap, his eyes blinking. "What's wrong?"

"There's been a twelve-car accident on the interstate. Massive injuries involved. That was my ER supervisor. They're desperate for staff and asked if I could possibly come to work by three o'clock to help out. I have to go," she explained to Cooper.

"Of course you do." He was rising and putting together their supplies. "I'll have you there by three, no problem. We'll ride double on Duke and make it back home, then I'll drive you."

"Thanks, Cooper. But just get me to the ranch as fast as you can. It's gonna be a very late night, so I'd better drive myself into Dallas. I have no idea when I'll get off."

He looked like he wanted to argue, but finally gave his head a nod and, in less than five minutes, she was seated in front of Cooper on his big stallion, her horse trailing behind, and racing back to Stone Ridge.

"Oh, crap, Katy," Lauren said into her car speakerphone. "I totally forgot about my appointment with the florist and photographer."

"Yes, you did. After they drove all the way out to the ranch, they called me to complain," Katy answered. "And they didn't hold back. It wasn't pretty. What's going on with you, Lauren?"

"I'm so sorry, Katy. After you went to all the trouble to seek them out and make the appointments for me, I don't know what to say. I'm wrapped up in something right now. It's crazy, but I don't have time to tell you. I'm on my way home from Dallas Memorial and I'm dragging. You heard about the big accident on the interstate? They called me in to help out today."

"Is that your excuse? Because it's a good one. Who could argue with that? You were saving lives. You were, weren't you?"

"Yes. We did help a lot of patients today. Thank goodness, most of the injuries were minor and we sent more than twenty patients home after treating them. There're a few who are in surgery right now and the others will probably be released by tomorrow morning. So, they let me go earlier than expected. I'm driving back to Cooper's now. But, Katy, I have to be honest with you. It wasn't the accident that made me miss my appointments today."

"Oh, boy, I think I know what's coming. Cooper?"

"Yes," she said without hesitation. "I'm in love with him, Katy."

"I figured. I mean he's…never mind. What about the fact that you're still engaged to Roger? Or are you?"

"Not in my heart and I am not wearing his ring anymore. I can't break up with him over the phone and I can't text him. I need to see him face-to-face and tell him everything up front."

"Okay, I gotta say I agree with that. So you don't want me to reschedule those appointments?"

"No. Sorry. And I promise to explain all of this to you tomorrow. But I'm exhausted now and almost at the ranch, so please don't do or say anything until we talk."

"I want details."

"You'll get them, I promise. I've gotta go. Pulling into the gates now. 'Bye, awesome friend. Love ya."

"Love ya, too."

As tired as she was, Lauren couldn't wait to see

Cooper and tell him about the day she'd had. She parked her car in one of the many garages attached to the house and noticed that Jared's luxurious red Lamborghini was parked inside, too. It was nine o'clock and they were probably just finishing up dinner. As much as she wanted to see Cooper, she didn't want to interrupt his private time with his brother. Maybe she'd just pop her head into the room and say good-night to them.

She needed her Cooper Stone fix.

And then she could crash in her bed.

As she entered the house, she noticed the kitchen lights were off. Voices drifted inside from the backyard patio. A few Malibu lights cast a dim glow over the area. It was peaceful, soothing her nerves. She was about to walk outside when she heard her name mentioned.

She froze, hiding herself from view in the dark kitchen. Jared was speaking loud enough for her to hear. And he sounded irritated. "You told me you weren't getting involved with her. You had no feelings for Lauren."

"I know all that," Cooper retorted, clearly upset. "What was I supposed to do? Loretta asked me to stop the wedding and I didn't expect it would end up like this."

"What, with you banging your best friend's sister?"

"Shut the hell up, Jared. Not another word about Lauren, you hear me."

"Hey, no disrespect to her. Lauren's great. Maybe too great. That's my point. You were doomed from the beginning."

"That doesn't change the fact that Tony thought Kelsey was robbing him blind. As soon as Tony was gone, the guy tries to cement the deal by marrying his partner's sister. It's a good way to cover his tracks *and* keep the company for himself."

"We have no proof of that. I couldn't find anything on Tony's computer."

"Something's up with that Winding Hills Resort. If we could break into Kelsey's files at his office, we'd find our proof there. I'm sure of it. We have to…"

Lauren's ears were burning. Her heart was crushed, battering her chest with each beat. This was too much to take in. She questioned if she was too exhausted to be hearing this correctly, but she knew. She'd heard right. Cooper had betrayed her in the worst possible way. He'd taken her trust, her love, her body, and used her.

Oh, man. Oh, man. Oh, man.

"We can't do that," Jared said firmly. "That's breaking and entering."

"Hell, I know that. I wish I'd never gotten involved in this scheme."

Blood drained from Lauren's face. Her body sagged. She felt as weak as one of her geriatric patients. Her head hurt like hell from the truth that pounded at her like a freaking sledgehammer.

Cooper doesn't love you.

He doesn't care about you.

He was paying a debt he thought he owed your mother.

To ease his guilt about Tony.

He seduced you with his charm and good looks.

And, Mama! Why didn't you trust me with the truth? Did you think I'm so much of a flake that you had to go behind my back to cook up a scheme with Cooper? Didn't you know it would completely shatter me that you showed so little faith in my judgment?

Lauren stood there shaking. Her brain should have been muddled. Heartbreak combined with fatigue had a way of doing that. But suddenly her mind opened and all things became clear. The tears would come later and they would be massive. She had no doubt she was ruined for life. She'd never love again. She'd never trust again. She'd been duped by a master deceiver. Make that two.

She walked out onto the patio and both men turned their heads, shocked to see her there. The Stone brothers swallowed hard and blinked. They couldn't believe their eyes. They'd been caught red-handed.

Hell, yeah.

The pain squeezing her heart so tight she could barely breathe suddenly turned to white-hot anger.

"Lauren!" Cooper stood, taking a step to approach her.

She raised the palm of her hand, stopping him cold. Then she summoned every ounce of her strength. "Don't. Don't you dare come any closer. Don't you dare speak to me, Cooper Stone."

"Maybe I should leave," Jared said, standing, his expression as grim as Cooper's.

"Don't bother, Jared. I won't be here that long."

"I can explain," Cooper said. The alarm in his voice didn't faze her.

"I don't need your lies, Cooper. I don't think there's anything left to say. I heard it all. You and my mother cooked up this scheme to break up my engagement. And you did a bang-up job. Leave it to you, Cooper, you always have to win. You love a challenge. And that's all I was to you, right? Well, I'll tell you one thing. Your plan didn't work. I'm *not* breaking up with my fiancé. I'm marrying Roger and I won't hear an-other word about it." The loud and intense pain in her voice carried across the patio. Had she just said that? Yeah, she had. To hurt Cooper. To get back at him for deceiving and using her. For breaking her heart.

"Lauren, you can't be serious!"

"Don't get indignant with me, Cooper." Tears streamed down her face. Tremors racked her body so hard she almost lost her balance. She gripped the wall to steady herself. "My mind is made up. I'm going through with the wedding."

She started walking away. Out of the corner of her eye, she saw Cooper taking a step to come after her. Jared hooked his arm and held him back. "Not now," Jared said. "She needs time to cool off."

Cool off? She would never cool off. She was ice from now on.

She headed upstairs to her room and quickly packed her bag. She needed to get off this ranch and away from Cooper Stone, yesterday.

She needed a place to cry her eyes out.

She needed to go home.

Nine

Lauren woke in her own bed from a fitful sleep just as the first dawn light settled upon the world. She hugged her tear-soaked pillow tight. Last night her sobs had come steadily until she was too drained to do anything but fall into an exhausted sleep. She propped herself up in bed, took a few moments to clear her head and rose. Immediately she wished she could flop back down and cover her head with her blanket. Stay there until life made sense again.

As if.

The aroma of freshly brewed coffee teased her nostrils.

She headed to the kitchen and stared at her mama sitting at the table, sipping from her Nursing Is a Work of Heart coffee mug. Her mouth was turned down and worry lines surrounded her bloodshot eyes.

Lauren poured herself a cup and sat facing her. She had burning questions for her mother, and tried not to think of her as Benedict Arnold. Yet she did feel totally betrayed. "How long have the painters been gone?" she asked quietly.

"Just since yesterday, honey."

"At least that wasn't a lie. The house is painted inside and out."

"I was going to tell you today."

"Was all that about Sadie a lie, too?"

"No, honey," her mama said. "You think I'd lie about something like that?"

No. Not really. But it all seemed too convenient and it had left Lauren alone with Cooper at Stone Ridge. She shook her head. "How is she?"

"Better. She's home with 'round-the-clock care."

"That's good." Lauren took a big sip of coffee and it went down hard. "Mama, why did you do it? Didn't you know it would crush me to find out how little you trusted me? It was like a slap in the face."

Her mama reached for her hand. She wasn't ready to give in to the gesture, but the sense of loss in her mother's eyes was the same look she'd had when Tony died. And Lauren couldn't do that to her. She couldn't turn her mother's hand away.

Her mother squeezed her hand gently. "I'm sorry. I was desperate. Honey, I know you don't like to hear this, but you've been impulsive in the past, and with your brother only being gone a short time, I thought you were making a big mistake rushing into marriage. You needed time to grieve and get your life back in order. I didn't want to break you and Roger up, as much as have you give yourself more time. I thought that moving to the ranch would help you clear your head a bit. Distance can help give you perspective. And then maybe you'd see that Roger was pushing you too hard."

"You mean you wanted to separate me from Roger any way you could. And you asked Cooper to help you do that."

"It just all sort of happened, honey. Look, it's no surprise to anyone that I made a mistake marrying your father. He wasn't a man made for settling down. I didn't want that to happen to you."

Lauren stared into her coffee cup. "I guess I'm just like Dad."

"No, honey. You are not like him at all. You're a nurturer. You're kind. And thoughtful. You care deeply about people. I just wanted you to understand your own heart, without being pressured into marrying a man who maybe wasn't right for you."

"Well, you succeeded. You pushed me toward Cooper."

"You have to know that was never my intention or his, honey. Cooper isn't that devious."

Again, her mama was defending Cooper. He was a saint. Saint Cooper could do no wrong. But her mother had no idea how much Cooper's betrayal cut into her, slicing her to pieces. Had he seduced her, made love to her, because he'd run out of other options? Had he deliberately set out to ruin her for Roger and all other men?

"Mama, I'm a mess inside. I'm questioning all my decisions."

"Oh, honey. I'm so very sorry about that. I didn't mean for any of this to happen." She rose. "Come here, baby girl." She opened her arms.

Lauren got up and moved into her mother's embrace. She felt safe there, comforted by her mother's love. "Lauren, I'm sorry. I hope you can forgive me, honey. The last thing I want is for you to be hurt."

"Oh, Mama." It was too late for that.

"Cooper's worried sick about you, honey. He's been calling. He sounded pretty desperate to talk to you."

"No."

"No?"

She pulled out of her mother's arms. "Mama, no. I…can't. I'm furious with him and I don't think that's going to change. You don't know the half of it."

"I think I do. You care deeply about him."

So, her mama was perceptive. That wasn't a big shocker. "Cared. Past tense. I don't want to talk about Cooper. But just for the record, right now the way I feel about him is something just short of…loathing."

"It's not his fault, honey. I shouldn't have gone behind your back to seek his help."

"What is it about that man that you're always defending him? He doesn't walk on water, you know."

"He's a good man, and I put him in a terrible situation."

"Cooper did what he always does, going above and beyond to accomplish his goals. And I fell for it. Like a fool."

"You're no fool, Lauren. You're a girl with a big heart."

"Please, Mama, promise me one thing?"

"Anything, Lauren. I want to earn back your trust."

"No matter what I decide to do, promise me I'll have your support. You'll stand by my decision and not try to interfere."

"Oh, Lauren. I've learned my lesson. I promise. I do trust you, baby girl. And I love you with all of my heart."

"Love you, too, Mama."

Lauren stood at the reception desk at Kelsey-Abbott, dressed in a cream pencil skirt and a light cocoa blouse. Her three-inch heels were killing her, but it didn't matter. She'd withstand the pain as long as she got what she came here to find. She waved to a few employees she recognized from Tony's days at the company and was granted kind greetings back.

With Katy by her side, she said to the new twenty-something receptionist, "I'm Lauren Abbott, Mr. Kelsey's fiancée. I need to get into Roger's office." She smiled brightly, and rather than plead her case that she had every right to be there, she was half owner of the company, she took an easier route. "I'm afraid I lost a diamond earring in there. It's sort of special since he gave me the pair on my birthday. I'm hoping I can find it before he returns from his trip tomorrow and then I won't have to admit to him I'd been a little careless with his gift."

"Sure. No problem, Miss Abbott," the young woman

said, giving her a look of sympathy. "Would you like some help looking for it?"

"That's very sweet of you—" Lauren glanced at the name on her badge "—Melissa. But that's not necessary. It's lunchtime and I don't want to hold you up. I brought my friend Katy with me. She's got eagle eyes. If anyone can help me find it, it's her."

"That's right," Katy said. "Needle in the haystack and all."

The receptionist furrowed her brows, looking ridiculously puzzled. Clearly she was clueless as to what Katy meant. "Well, let me find the keys," she said, opening a drawer and coming up with a key ring. "Would you like me to show you in?"

"No, thanks," Lauren answered, snapping up the keys. "I've got this." She waved the key ring in the air as she headed toward the office. "Have a great lunch, Melissa."

"I hope you find what you're looking for."

"So do I," Lauren mumbled under her breath.

Once they were inside Roger's office, Katy turned the lock on the door and simultaneously their shoulders sagged. "Wow," she said.

"Technically, we're not doing anything wrong. I own half of this company."

"I never understood how that worked. If you're not involved in the company, how do you know you're earning your fair share?"

"Up until now, I had no reason to think Roger was cheating Tony or me."

Lauren had come up with her plan last night, amid

all the sobs and heartache, and was determined to find out what kind of man Roger Kelsey actually was. He'd been attentive to her after Tony's death and, okay, maybe she'd let her guard down enough to think she'd fallen in love with him. But it seemed that as soon as the engagement ring was on her finger, he'd backed off. As if she was a sure thing. As if his mission had been accomplished. The more she'd thought about how Roger so eagerly pursued her after the funeral, the more she was beginning to believe that what she'd overheard last night between Jared and Cooper was true.

Not that it would let Cooper Stone off the hook.

This morning, after confronting and finally, for the most part, forgiving her mother, she'd driven over to Katy's house and spilled her heart out, leaving no details unspoken. Katy knew everything and it was amazing how liberating that was now that the burden of secrecy had been lifted.

Lauren's phone buzzed. It was another text from Cooper. He'd sent her four already and left a couple of voice-mail messages, too. She hadn't bothered to listen to them. Her stomach knotted good and tight every time his name popped up on the screen, so she turned her phone off and dropped it into her handbag. If only she could turn her thoughts of him off that easily.

"Let's get started," she said to Katy. Finding out her fiancé was a cheat and possibly a fraud was a better option than thinking about Cooper's betrayal. Wasn't that just sad? She sure knew how to pick 'em. *Not*.

"You really think he'd leave something incriminating on his work computer?"

"I have no clue. Good thing I brought you along, right?" Katy was a techno wizard. She was one of those people who had worked with computers from a very young age, understanding the language better than some people understood English. Lauren was so on the other end of the spectrum. She excelled in most subjects, yet she didn't know a gigabyte from an internal hard drive. "My future is riding on this," she said, biting her nail.

"I'll try my best. But you know, you're within your legal right to have the books audited."

"And spoil all of our fun? No way, Katy. Besides, if Roger got wind of it, he'd have time to cook the books."

"Okay, well, let a girl get to work." Katy took a seat in Roger's chair and opened the computer.

"While you hunt for electronic clues, I'll go through the paper files. See if I can come up with something."

"Sounds good and, while you're at it, do me a favor?"

Her friend was a trooper, letting Lauren cry on her shoulder this morning and now attempting to hack into the company's computer for her. "Anything."

"Think about what you really want in life. And go after it."

"I promise, but first things first. I need to find out if my fiancé is true blue."

"And then what?"

A lump formed in her throat. Did she have the gumption to go through with her plan? She'd teach the two men in her life not to ever again mess with

Lauren Abbott. "Then if it goes as I think it will, I'll be walking down the aisle in ten days."

"I should've never let you stop me from going after her. I should've talked to her that night and made her see reason." Cooper sank onto the big leather sofa in his brother's game room and hung his head. It had been a whole week since he'd seen Lauren. "She won't answer my texts or phone calls."

"She's not ready yet," Jared said. "You would've only made things worse. She was seeing red that night and rightfully so."

"Are you gonna lecture me?" Cooper's head ached. He was in no mood to hear how badly he'd screwed up.

"No. Hey, remember, I was on the receiving end of a situation like this. Helene lied to me about who she was. Her motives didn't matter at the time. All I could see was her betrayal."

"Totally different situation. I'm not ready to let Lauren go. She can't marry that guy."

"Why not? We didn't find a thing on him."

"But it's there. Tony's instincts were always right on."

"Maybe, but it's out of your hands right now."

"It can't be."

"Why?"

"Why do you keep asking me why?" Cooper's head hammered harder now. He put his fingertips to the temples and massaged them to release some of the pressure. It wasn't working.

"Because you're not being honest with yourself."

"What do you want me to say?"

"The truth."

"Okay, I miss her. I miss her like crazy. And she deserves someone better than Roger Kelsey."

Jared pointed a finger right smack at his chest.

"Me? No way, Jared." He gave his head a shake. "It can't be me. I killed her brother. I could never expect her to love me that way. I don't deserve Lauren's love."

"Maybe she deserves yours. Did you ever think of it that way? I saw the look in her eyes that night she walked in on our conversation. She's crazy about you, Cooper. That's the reason she was so devastated. And would you stop with the I-killed-her-brother thing. You know you didn't. You know it wasn't you driving recklessly that night. In all your life, you've never had one accident. It was bad luck and timing that caused Tony's death. Stop blaming yourself."

"I'm tryin', bro. I'm tryin'."

"Well, try harder or you're gonna lose her forever."

Cooper's cell rang and his heart started pumping fast. Every time someone called, he held out hope it was Lauren coming to her senses. But this time he got the next best thing. "Excuse me," he told Jared. "It's Loretta." He hated hearing the eagerness in his voice. Maybe Loretta was calling with news of Lauren? Man, he was messed up. Clutching the phone tight, he rose from his seat, walked out front and sat on the stone steps.

"Hello, Loretta."

"Cooper. How are you?"

"I'm doing fine," he fibbed. "Well, just okay. I'm hoping you have good news to tell me about Lauren."

"Cooper, I'm actually calling on Lauren's behalf. I've promised my daughter to support her decision, no matter what it is. And I'm afraid she's decided to marry Roger. I couldn't even try to talk her out of it. I kept my mouth shut. She claims she knows what she's doing."

"It's clear that she doesn't."

"I can't help you, Cooper. I'm lucky she's even talking to me. She's been very hurt and I'm trying to earn back her trust."

Cooper's body sagged. Loretta was his last line of defense.

"She's in the other room. She said she'll speak to you, if you want to talk to her."

"I'd rather see her in person."

"Well, I can put her on the phone and let you ask her. It's really out of my hands."

"Okay, Loretta. I understand. Please put her on."

A minute passed and Cooper's throat tightened. He cleared it with a cough.

"Hello," Lauren said.

The sound of her sweet, lilting voice coming over the receiver melted his heart.

"Lauren." He pulled air into his lungs and sighed silently. She was like an angel, the only woman who could repair the pieces of him that were broken. How he'd missed her this past week. "I'm glad you agreed to speak to me. I want you to know—"

"You don't have to say anything. I know you're sorry. Mama's only told me a dozen times. But I can't hear your platitudes, Cooper. I thought I owed you a call to say I'm going through with my wedding."

Cooper slammed his eyes shut. He ground his teeth and summoned all of his patience "You can't marry him. He's a cheat and I can't stand the thought of you tying yourself to a man who doesn't deserve you."

"I know what kind of man Roger is, Cooper. And that's why I'm marrying him. I've done some digging on my own. I know you and Mama didn't think me capable, but I am."

"Are you saying—?"

"I'm saying that I'm a stronger, more competent woman than either of you gave me credit for. And that's all I'm going to say about it."

"Did you tell Roger about us?"

"Us?"

"Yeah, about you and me?"

"I told him I got a case of cold feet, Cooper. And I finally came to my senses."

Her words sunk in. So now what they'd had together boiled down to a case of cold feet on her part. Not that he'd given her any reason to think there was more to the relationship. He'd been too dense, too blind, felt too guilty to claim the woman he wanted. And now it was hopeless. She was set and determined to marry Kelsey.

She'd done some digging on her own and hadn't found anything. Kelsey wasn't about to leave his secrets to be easily found. Lauren couldn't have possibly dug deep enough, but apparently she was convinced Kelsey was innocent of any wrongdoing.

"I wanted to let you off the hook if you'd rather

we don't get married at Stone Ridge. Roger originally wanted to marry at the courthouse. He's all about simple," she said. "And, certainly, I would understand if you didn't want to host the wedding."

Cooper squeezed his eyes shut. Pain stabbed at him, a burning ache that rifled through his entire body. He wanted her on Stone Ridge. She belonged here. With him. If he told her what was in his heart, it would go over like a train wreck. She wouldn't believe him. She would only think he was meddling in her life again. But how could he let her go? How could he possibly give her away to another man?

Because this is what she wants.

You blew it with her.

The least you can do is let her have the wedding of her dreams.

"Lauren, are you sure? You're not just doing this because of what…what happened between us."

"You keep saying 'us' as if there is such a thing. There never was, Cooper. I made a mistake and now I'm trying to rectify it."

There was no anger or pain in her voice, and that was what scared him the most. He only heard determination.

"I made you a promise and regardless of what you think of me, I won't go back on my word. Everything is all set. So, if that's what you really want, you can certainly have the wedding here."

"I don't…" she said, her voice dropping to a whisper, giving him a sliver of hope. "I mean… I don't expect you to walk me down the aisle."

"No." He couldn't imagine it.

"But I do hope you'll attend the wedding."

He'd have to show up for Tony, for Loretta, for Lauren. "Yep." He all but strangled on the word.

"Thank you," she said quite civilly. "Goodbye, Cooper."

She cut off the connection and he just sat there, swallowing hard and staring at the phone.

Jared shoved a glass of whiskey into his free hand. "Here. You look like you could use this." Jared sat beside him on the stone steps, holding a crystal carafe of the good stuff.

"I need more than this." He gulped the shot.

"What you need is to grow some balls, Coop."

He frowned as he eyed his brother. "What?"

"You heard me. You're sulking around like a baby. Since when do you give up? You're a fierce competitor. Get in Lauren's face if you have to."

"It's too late. I spoke with her. She's marrying Roger. She says hooking up with me was only a case of cold feet."

"Do you believe that?"

"Hell, no."

"Then talk to her. Really talk to her. Spill out your guts and tell her how you feel. Offer her the moon. That's what women want. They want all of you, not just the parts you're willing to share."

Jared poured him another shot and he sipped slowly this time. "Thanks for the advice."

"You taking it?"

"I'm growing a pair, as we speak," Cooper said.

His brother chuckled. And, for the first time in days, so did he.

* * *

Katy finished buttoning the last of the pearl buttons at the back of Lauren's wedding dress. She stared at herself in the dresser mirror in Cooper's guest room, the room where she'd stayed just a short time ago. Her mother's ivory-silk gown had a vintage look about it. It was a dream dress for a dream wedding. Only that dream had turned into a bit of a nightmare. "Are you sure you want to go through with this, Lauren?"

Katy could tell she was freaking out, her nerves doing a hip-hop dance, up and down and sideways. "Yes, I have to."

"You don't. You can back out."

"I really can't and you know why."

"Then you're a braver woman than I am."

"My bravery might be born of stupidity, Katy. I can't go backward. I've got to see this through."

"Oh…kay."

Katy's obvious reluctance was working on her. Making her doubt her decision.

"You look gorgeous, BFF. You really do."

"Thanks."

"Just let me fix a few of these curls. Once your veil goes on, you'll be all done."

Katy got out the curling iron again and rewound a curl just as a soft knock sounded on the door. "That must be Mama. I'll get it," Lauren said.

Katy shook her head and touched Lauren's shoulders. "You just stay put right there, I'll get the door."

Lauren tilted her head and smiled.

"It's my duty as your maid of honor. And I take my duties seriously."

"I know you do."

Katy had been a godsend to her during this past month, helping her get her head on straight. Not an easy task, since she'd been turned upside down lately. She didn't know how she'd ever repay her for her support and kindness.

The door creaked open and she heard a familiar male voice. Cooper's. "I'd like to see Lauren."

Katy closed the door halfway. "Uh, hold on," she told him. Stunned, Katy turned around and waited for a sign from her.

Lauren froze. She thought she'd made it clear she didn't want to see him before the wedding. But she couldn't very well kick him to the curb, since she was in his house, having her wedding on his property. She was still angry with him, so angry she could barely see straight. But good manners prevailed. In a few minutes, none of this would matter anymore.

"Katy, I'll see him."

You sure? she mouthed.

She nodded.

Katy opened the door all the way and let him in. "I'll just go…check on our bouquets."

Lauren hadn't ended up hiring a florist or a photographer. The bouquets for her and Katy were last-minute indulgences from the Garden House in Dallas. Katy had picked them up this morning and put them in the refrigerator for safekeeping. Since the lake property was such a naturally beautiful setting, Lauren figured it was okay to forego any other flowers. As far as photography, a few friends had been asked to bring their good cameras. That would have to do, and given the circumstances of her little plan, it was more than enough.

Cooper waited until Katy was fully out of sight before coming farther into the room. Wearing a charcoal suit, his dark blond hair cut and groomed to perfection, and sexy facial scruff accenting his strong jawbone, he simply took her breath away. He held a felt hat over his heart.

"You look beautiful," were the first words out of his mouth, the sincerity of his comment shining in his deep, sea-blue eyes "I've missed you so much, Lauren."

She'd missed him, too, but she remained silent.

He took a few steps, closing in on her, and the look of fear on her face must've stopped him from coming any closer. He stood in the middle of the room now, staring at her. "I'm sorry about the way things happened, Lauren. Your mom only wanted what was best for you. And I blew it while trying to help."

She nodded, tears brimming in her eyes. Her mascara would be running any second and she'd look like the sister act to Kiss.

"I couldn't let you marry Kelsey without telling you how I feel about you. It may be too late, but I only just figured it out and…well, it's as simple as it is complicated, really. I'm in love with you, Lauren. I fell for you without even realizing it. In my heart, there is an 'us.' And I'm afraid there always will be. You probably don't believe me, but it's true. And I swear it on Tony's grave. I love you, Lauren."

Lauren put her head down, holding back tears. She stood in her wedding gown, her train flowing in a silky circle on the floor all around her. She wasn't a prize to be collected. She wasn't a flake or a fool. She knew what she wanted and she would have to see this through to the end. She looked up at Cooper through teary eyes. He'd been everything she'd ever wanted. "Thank you, Cooper."

"Thank you?" he repeated, an incredulous tone in his voice.

"Yes, I appreciate your honesty. I really do."

Cooper's hopeful expression vanished and was quickly replaced by a frown. "So that's it?"

Oh, God. Why was he doing this to her? As angry as she'd been with him, she didn't relish hurting him. "I… I have to get my veil and bouquet. The w-wedding will be starting soon."

"I'd like to shake some sense into you," he said quietly. "But I don't think it would help."

If he touched her, she would crumble and she couldn't have that. "No. It wouldn't."

Slowly, he set his hat on his head. "Then I hope you get what you're looking for."

She nodded.

He walked toward the door and reached for the knob.

She called to him, "Cooper, you're still coming, right?"

His nod was barely visible. But it was there. And

once he stepped out of the room, her shoulders fell and she breathed a big sigh of relief.

Lauren sat in the back of the Jeep with Katy, Jared Stone at the wheel. The seats were draped with soft cotton blankets to keep their gowns from getting dirty. "You both look dazzling," Jared said cordially. "I'll make it a smooth ride up to the lake."

"Thanks, Jared." Lauren's stomach was in knots. She prayed her wedding plans would go off without a hitch.

"Yes, I would appreciate that," Katy said. "I've got to keep this bride intact until the big reveal."

Jared nodded. "Noted."

Lauren rolled her eyes at her maid of honor's bad choice of words, but Katy only giggled, taking her hand and reassuring her now that the time had come.

"Most of the guests have already arrived," Jared informed them. "I saw the groom with his best man, just a little while ago. Cooper drove your mama up. So everything's set."

The air grew chilly and Lauren glanced at the sky. Threatening clouds gathered overhead. *Wonderful.*

"Let's get this show on the road," Katy said, shivering.

Jared started the engine and drove away from the house. Considering that Cooper's brother loved speed and power, driving the Jeep at a snail's pace was very thoughtful of him. The drive took just a few minutes. He parked at the canopied tent designated for the bridal party. Off in the distance, Lauren spotted chairs with big white bows tied around the backs, lined up in rows under the leafy oak tree. The guests were milling around, not yet in their seats.

"Here we are," Jared said, taking her hand and helping her down, then doing the same for Katy. "I'd better run, it's almost time." He gave them each a kiss on the cheek. "See you both later."

"He's awfully…nice," Katy said.

Katy's definition of nice meant hot and hunky.

Westward Movement started playing a soft, classical number and Katy took her cue. "Looks like we're on." She hugged Lauren gently, so as not to wrinkle her gown, and then set the bouquet of white roses and lilies in her hands. "Here you go." She sighed. "You're doing the right thing, honey."

"I think so, too."

"And remember, I'm right here if you need me."

"I know." Lauren blew her a kiss and Katy, dressed in a pale pink off-the-shoulder gown, started her twenty-yard march toward the gathered guests.

Lauren stepped out of the tent and began walking slowly, her arms shivering now, from both nerves and the chill in the air. She was halfway to the altar when something caught her eye. A white, heart-shaped, wooden sign that she'd never noticed before was planted in the ground. She took a few more steps and was able to read the print in italic red lettering.

Lake Laurie Loo

And underneath, the words,

Forever and Always

Her throat closed up. Tears brimmed in her eyes. She stopped to catch her breath as her heart dipped into oblivion. First, Cooper had appeared and declared his love while she was dressing, and now this. If he was trying to make a point, he was succeeding.

Out of the corner of her eye she spotted him standing rigid, several feet away from the back row as if he was attending the ceremony, but not really. *Dear God.* Swallowing hard, she willed her feet to begin moving again and once she spotted Roger up at the altar smiling, patiently waiting next to his best buddy, Jonathan, she focused on him, only him.

When she reached the last row of chairs she halted and immediately the band's rendition of the "Wedding March" began playing.

Slowly, she began her walk down the aisle, passing rows and rows of guests standing and smiling at her, some teary-eyed. Katy's brother, Pete, and her plus one, gave Lauren a wink as she strode by. Approaching the front row, she found her mother's loving gaze on her. Her mama was trying to hide her disappointment by giving her a nod of encouragement, but Lauren wasn't fooled.

No one would fool her again.

She turned to give Katy her bouquet and then placed her hands in Roger's.

"Are you ready for this?" he whispered.

"Oh, so ready," she answered.

Minister Patterson cleared his throat and began the

ceremony. Roger wanted to keep things light and simple, so after the minister spoke about the sanctity of marriage and their duties to one another, he began the ring ceremony. Roger said a few words about their future and then placed the gold band on her finger.

Lauren did the same, her hands trembling as she pushed the ring onto Roger's left hand. He gazed down at her and smiled.

"And now, if anyone knows of a reason this couple should not be joined in holy matrimony, let them speak now or forever hold their peace."

The guests sat quietly. Not even a whisper could be heard. And then there was a crunching sound as boots hit the white runner. Lauren didn't have to turn around to know Cooper was there. Her heart pounded.

But this was hers to do and nothing was going to stop her.

"Me," she said, pulling her hands free as if Roger's were on fire. She backed away from him, "I am speaking now, Minister Patton. I cannot marry this man."

The minister's eyes narrowed. "Excuse me, Lauren. Do you know what you're saying?"

She turned partially around to gaze at the invited guests. They had stunned looks on their faces. Then she caught sight of Cooper, standing there halfway up the aisle, equally stunned.

"Yes, I know exactly what I'm saying. I have every reason to believe that Roger Kelsey had been cheating my brother Tony, his loyal partner of many years, from funds due him. And now, as half owner in the company, he is also cheating me. Furthermore, upon inspection of his secret company tallies, I've determined he's been using that money to bribe officials down in Houston to gain favor for a multimillion dollar project."

"Now, wait a minute, Lauren. You don't know what you're talking about!"

"I most certainly do. Winding Hills Resort. We found evidence, Roger. You didn't think I was smart enough to figure it out. But I did, with some help. The only reason you're marrying me is so you can get your greedy hands on my half of the company and cover your ass. Well, that's not happening, buddy."

He reached for her hand. "Lauren, wait. This is all a misunderstanding. You can't be serious," he whispered through gritted teeth. "Stop this right now."

"I am stopping this." She wrestled the ring off her finger and plopped it into his hand. "If you were the last man on earth, I wouldn't marry you. You cheated your friend, Roger. Tony trusted you. I'm only glad we were able to uncover the truth and let all these people see what kind of a man you really are."

Just then, Katy's brother appeared, coming up the aisle, approaching them. "This is Officer Pete Millhouse with the Dallas Police Department. I believe he's got some questions for you."

Roger's reddened face got a horrified look. "You bitch," he growled just as thunder boomed, shaking the sky. It was fitting, this monstrous sound intensifying the moment. "You've got nothing on me."

"Mr. Kelsey, I'd like you to come down to the station to answer some questions." Pete's voice was forceful enough to sway Roger.

His shoulders slumped and he heaved a big sigh. "I want my lawyer."

"You have every right to contact your attorney." Office Millhouse escorted Roger away from the lake area where he met up with two uniformed officers.

Many of Roger's half of the wedding guests began getting up and leaving, mumbling under their breath. She hated to do this, hated to put these innocent people through such an ordeal, but not enough to stop her little plan. She felt guilty about that, but Roger deserved to be exposed for the fraud that he was.

His best man, Jonathan, gave her a scathing look and called her a vile name before exiting the area.

Lauren gazed out at the remaining guests, her friends, her family, her coworkers. Their astonished expressions would be ingrained in her memory forever.

"I love you all for coming to my faux wedding and I'm very sorry to put you through that. I hope you can forgive me for the theatrics. It's something I felt compelled to do."

Roger needed to be taught a lesson. He was a first-class creep and not only had he been cheating her, he'd been cheating *on* her with his secretary. They'd found evidence of that, too—tasteless bikini underwear hidden in one of Roger's suit pockets in his office closet. It was laughable really, how inept he thought Lauren was, but underestimating her had been his downfall. She'd uncovered the truth, for her brother, and now she was free of Roger Kelsey forever.

"Lauren." Cooper's powerful voice commanded her attention. She turned and faced him, and his bluer-than-blue eyes penetrated every crevice of her heart. "This doesn't have to be a fake wedding."

"Cooper, what are you saying?"

"I'm saying, I love you." He spoke loud enough for all of the remaining guests to hear. "I love you so much, I was about to make a fool out of myself and stop this wedding myself. Luckily, you spared me that, but Lauren Camille Abbott, know this. You are my heart and soul, and I can't imagine my life without you. I'm sorry for all the pain I've caused you. So very sorry."

"You lied to me, Cooper Stone," she said firmly. Cooper needed to be taught a lesson, too. But then she remembered how earnest he'd been declaring his love earlier. And naming the lake in her honor had earned him half a dozen brownie points, too.

"I'll never do that again."

"You deceived me and that hurt."

Heads ping-ponged back and forth with each new twist in the conversation. At least Lauren knew how to entertain her guests.

"I'll spend my life making it up to you."

The crowd muttered sympathetic ahs.

Katy rushed up and pushed the bouquet back into her hands.

Jared walked over to stand beside Cooper on the white aisle runner.

A few guests began to applaud. Then a few more started clapping and, like a wave building and growing, the applause grew louder and more pronounced. Before she knew what was happening, Cooper was approaching her. "What do you say, Lauren? We have friends and family surrounding us and everything else we need to make this your dream wedding. Marry me today. You can forgive me another time."

Lauren glanced down at her mama, sitting with her hand to her mouth, waiting, hoping, praying. Good Lord, Lauren would never hear the end of it if she didn't say yes to this beautiful, wonderful, generous man, who made her absolutely crazy. "I've already forgiven you."

"You have?" His eyes sparked and hope stole over his expression as he walked to her side and took her hands in his. His touch reached deep down inside her.

She nodded, holding his hands, "Naming the lake after me pretty much sealed the deal. But, Cooper, I mean it. You can't go behind my back like that ever again. I need to trust you."

"I promise."

"He promises," her mother repeated.

Oh, for heaven's sake. Lauren smiled, finally free of all doubt and worry. He smiled back, and it was good and right and meant to be. "Cooper Stone. I love you with all my heart. Your sincere declaration of love in the dressing room convinced me how very much you mean to me. And I will admit, but don't get cocky about this, that if you hadn't intervened, I might've married that…that loser. So for that, I am grateful."

"I won't get cocky," he said. "Well, not until later," he whispered for her ears only.

A rush of heat rose up from her throat. She couldn't wait until later.

"Lauren Camille Abbott, I've never met a more

beautiful, intelligent, caring person in my life. You're perfect in every way and I've waited for you my entire life. Will you marry me right here on Stone Ridge?" he asked more formally now.

"Yes, Cooper Stone, I will marry you today."

Cooper squeezed her hands and closed his eyes, taking a deep breath. "Thank you." He turned to the pastor. "Minister Patterson, please do us the honor of marrying us in front of our family and friends."

"Well," he began, clearing his throat, "this is highly irregular."

"I know, but it's meant to be," Cooper insisted. "And the right thing for us." When he turned back to her, his eyes were filled with love.

The minister gave them a stern look. "Are you both absolutely sure?"

They nodded.

"You'll have to arrange the legalities of the union at a later date."

"We will. We only care what's in our hearts right now," Lauren said.

Cooper nodded. "That's right. So please, get on with the hitching."

"Very well." The minister turned to the crowd. "Ladies and gentlemen, it looks like we're having a wedding, after all."

Lightning flashed just over the rise and then the clouds overhead nudged each other. Within seconds, a light drizzle of rain floated down onto the ceremony.

Lauren put out her palms, capturing a few drops. Cooper laughed, throwing his head back.

And then she had a thought. "Maybe it's Tony, giving us his sign of approval."

"Couldn't be anything else," Cooper agreed.

"I've heard getting married in the rain brings the bride and groom good luck for years to come," Lauren said sweetly.

Cooper placed her hand over his heart as drops continued to fall from the sky. "I figure rain or shine, any day when you become my wife is my lucky day, Laurie Loo."

Cooper sat on the grass with Lauren beside him, facing Tony's grave. One raspberry-jelly doughnut sat on a napkin atop the headstone. Powdered sugar covered Lauren's hands and she licked at her fingers one at a time. "Mmm, this is so good, Coop."

"Being as you're wearing it, I guess so." He smiled at his wife, leaned over and wiped a clump of raspberry jelly off her cheek.

"I can see why my brother liked these. He always had a sweet tooth."

"Yep, these were his favorite."

The sky was clear and blue with a fresh bite in the air. It was about as beautiful a day as Cooper could ever remember, except for that day three months ago when he'd married Lauren.

He gobbled up the last of his doughnut and flipped the lid on the box, going in for his second one.

"Careful, honey. You don't want to gain doughnut weight," she teased.

"Doughnut weight?" His brows lifted. "Sweetheart, I've never heard of that."

"No? But you've heard of baby weight, right?" she asked.

He stared at her, nodding his head. It was a strange statement. Where was she going with this? "Yeah."

"And so you won't mind if I put on a few pounds. For our baby?"

For our baby.

Cooper blinked, once, twice, and then he nearly lost it. "Our baby?"

Lauren nodded and a sweet smile spread across her face, the look in her eyes gooey-soft. "I'm pregnant, Cooper."

Tears welled in his eyes and his heart nearly burst from his chest. Overcome with emotion, he took her into his arms—a little clumsily, since they were sitting cross-legged—and kissed her senseless. "I can't believe it. I surely can't believe it. When is the baby due?"

"I'm about two months along, Coop."

He placed a hand on her belly, where their child grew. His child, with Lauren. The most perfect woman in the world was going to have his baby. He had a lot to measure up to. His father had left some pretty big shoes to fill, too. "I'm...going to try to be a good daddy to our child," he said reverently. "I promise."

"I have no doubt you will be." Lauren touched his cheek.

"You're gonna be a fantastic mother." Lauren was a nurturer, a woman with a heart as big as Texas. All that nonsense about her being unable to commit had washed away the minute they'd fallen in love. She'd just been waiting for the right man to come along. Him. And now their child would be blessed with her love, too.

"Thank you, Coop. I thought you and Tony should hear the news together."

Thick emotion clogged his throat. "It's fitting."

"I think he'd be happy you knocked up his little sister."

Cooper shook his head, but grinned like a damn fool. Lauren was a tease and a brat and the absolute love of his life. "Yeah, I think Tony would approve."

Cooper had come a long way in just a few months. He no longer blamed himself for the accident. He'd been set free of guilt and he had Lauren to thank for that. She'd taught him how to forgive himself and how to move on. Now, they were starting a family.

"Mama is going to go ballistic when we tell her the good news."

"Same with my mother," he said. She'd forgiven him for getting married without telling her. It wasn't exactly how he'd planned on marrying Lauren. But his mother had come to their civil ceremony, making their marriage legal and binding, the following week, and that seemed to appease her. "Mom's gonna love being a grandmother. She may even move back to Dallas."

The wind kicked up and Lauren shivered. "Take me home, Cooper," she said, grabbing his hand. "I'm having a craving."

"What would you like? You've already had a jelly doughnut."

"My craving isn't for food, silly. I want to cuddle up against the man I love and just be."

"Just be what, sweetheart?"

"Mrs. Cooper Stone, wife and soon-to-be mommy."

"I like the sound of that, Laurie Loo. Let's go home to Stone Ridge."

* * * * *

*Don't miss Jared Stone's story,
coming Fall 2018!*

*If you liked this story of family and passion,
pick up these other novels from*
USA TODAY *bestselling author Charlene Sands!*

*SUNSET SURRENDER
SUNSET SEDUCTION
THE SECRET HEIR OF SUNSET RANCH
ONE SECRET NIGHT, ONE SECRET BABY
TWINS FOR THE TEXAN
THE TEXAN'S ONE-NIGHT STANDOFF*

Available now from Harlequin Desire!

* * *

*If you're on Twitter,
tell us what you think of Harlequin Desire!
#harlequindesire*

COMING NEXT MONTH FROM

HARLEQUIN®

Desire

Available May 1, 2018

#2587 AN HONORABLE SEDUCTION

The Westmoreland Legacy • by Brenda Jackson

Navy SEAL David "Flipper" Holloway has one mission: get close to gorgeous store owner Swan Jamison and find out all he can. But flirtation leads to seduction and he's about to get caught between duty and the woman he vows to claim as his...

#2588 REUNITED...WITH BABY

Texas Cattleman's Club: The Impostor • by Sara Orwig

Wealthy tech tycoon Luke has come home and he'll do whatever it takes to revive his family's ranch. Even hire the woman he left behind, veterinarian and single mother Scarlett. He can't say yes to forever, but will one more night be enough?

#2589 THE TWIN BIRTHRIGHT

Alaskan Oil Barons • by Catherine Mann

When reclusive inventor Royce Miller is reunited with his ex-fiancée and her twin babies in a snowstorm, he vows to protect them at all costs—even if the explosive chemistry that drove them apart is stronger than ever!

#2590 THE ILLEGITIMATE BILLIONAIRE

Billionaires and Babies • by Barbara Dunlop

Black sheep Deacon Holt, illegitimate son of a billionaire, must marry the gold-digging widow of his half brother if he wants his family's recognition. Actually desiring the beautiful single mother isn't part of the plan, especially when she has shocking relevations of her own...

#2591 WRONG BROTHER, RIGHT MAN

Switching Places • by Kat Cantrell

To inherit his fortune, flirtatious Valentino LeBlanc must swap roles with his too-serious brother. He'll prove he's just as good as, if not better than, his brother. At everything. But when he hires his brother's ex to advise him, things won't stay professional for long...

#2592 ONE NIGHT TO FOREVER

The Ballantyne Billionaires • by Joss Wood

When Lachlyn is outed as a long-lost Ballantyne heiress, wealthy security expert Reame vows to protect her. She's his best friend's sister, an innocent... Surely he can keep his hands to himself. But all it takes is one night to ignite a passion that could burn them both...

Get 2 Free Books,
Plus 2 Free Gifts—
just for trying the Reader Service!

YES! Please send me 2 FREE Harlequin® Desire novels and my 2 FREE gifts (gifts are worth about $10 retail). After receiving them, if I don't wish to receive any more books, I can return the shipping statement marked "cancel." If I don't cancel, I will receive 6 brand-new novels every month and be billed just $4.55 per book in the U.S. or $5.24 per book in Canada. That's a savings of at least 13% off the cover price! It's quite a bargain! Shipping and handling is just 50¢ per book in the U.S. and 75¢ per book in Canada*. I understand that accepting the 2 free books and gifts places me under no obligation to buy anything. I can always return a shipment and cancel at any time. The free books and gifts are mine to keep no matter what I decide.

225/326 HDN GMWG

Name (PLEASE PRINT)

Address   Apt. #

City   State/Prov.   Zip/Postal Code

Signature (if under 18, a parent or guardian must sign)

Mail to the **Reader Service:**
IN U.S.A.: P.O. Box 1341, Buffalo, NY 14240-8531
IN CANADA: P.O. Box 603, Fort Erie, Ontario L2A 5X3

Want to try two free books from another line?
Call 1-800-873-8635 or visit www.ReaderService.com.

*Terms and prices subject to change without notice. Prices do not include applicable taxes. Sales tax applicable in N.Y. Canadian residents will be charged applicable taxes. Offer not valid in Quebec. This offer is limited to one order per household. Books received may not be as shown. Not valid for current subscribers to Harlequin Desire books. All orders subject to approval. Credit or debit balances in a customer's account(s) may be offset by any other outstanding balance owed by or to the customer. Please allow 4 to 6 weeks for delivery. Offer available while quantities last.

Your Privacy—The Reader Service is committed to protecting your privacy. Our Privacy Policy is available online at www.ReaderService.com or upon request from the Reader Service.

We make a portion of our mailing list available to reputable third parties that offer products we believe may interest you. If you prefer that we not exchange your name with third parties, or if you wish to clarify or modify your communication preferences, please visit us at www.ReaderService.com/consumerschoice or write to us at Reader Service Preference Service, P.O. Box 9062, Buffalo, NY 14240-9062. Include your complete name and address.

HD17R3

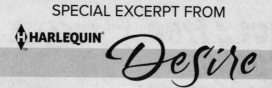
That damn buzz passed from him to her and ignited the flames low in her belly.

"When I get back to the office, you will officially become a client," Reame said in a husky voice. "But you're not my client…yet."

His words made no sense, but she did notice that he was looking at her like he wanted to kiss her.

Reame gripped her hips. She felt his heat and… Wow…

God and heaven.

Teeth scraped and lips soothed, tongues swirled and whirled, and heat, lazy heat, spread through her limbs and slid into her veins. Reame was kissing her, and time and space shifted.

It felt natural for her legs to wind around his waist, to lock her arms around his neck and take what she'd been fantasizing about. Kissing Reame was better than she'd imagined—she was finally experiencing all those fuzzy feels romance books described.

It felt perfect. It felt right.

Reame jerked his mouth off hers and their eyes connected, his intense, blazing with hot green fire.

She wanted him… She never wanted anybody. And never this much.

"Holy crap—"

Reame stiffened in her arms and Lachlyn looked over his shoulder to the now-open door to where her brother stood, half in and half out of the room. Lachlyn slid down Reame's hard body. She pushed her bangs off her forehead and released a deep breath, grateful that Reame shielded her from Linc.

Lachlyn touched her swollen lips and glanced down at her chest, where her hard nipples pushed against the fabric of her lacy bra and thin T-shirt. She couldn't possibly look more turned-on if she tried.

Lachlyn couldn't look at her brother, but he sounded thoroughly amused. "Want me to go away and come back in fifteen?"

Reame looked at her and, along with desire, she thought she saw regret in his eyes. He slowly shook his head. "No, we're done."

Lachlyn met his eyes and nodded her agreement.

Yes, they were done. They had to be.

Don't miss
ONE NIGHT TO FOREVER by Joss Wood,
*part of her **BALLANTYNE BILLIONAIRES** series!*

Available May 2018 wherever
Harlequin® Desire books and ebooks are sold.

www.Harlequin.com

Want to give in to temptation with
steamy tales of irresistible desire?

Check out **Harlequin® Presents®**,
Harlequin® Desire and
Harlequin® Kimani™ Romance books!

New books available every month!

CONNECT WITH US AT:

Harlequin.com/Community

 Facebook.com/HarlequinBooks

Twitter.com/HarlequinBooks

Instagram.com/HarlequinBooks

Pinterest.com/HarlequinBooks

ReaderService.com

HARLEQUIN®

**ROMANCE WHEN
YOU NEED IT**

PGENRE2017

LOVE
Harlequin
romance?

Join our Harlequin community to share your thoughts and connect with other romance readers!

Be the first to find out about promotions, news, and exclusive content!

Sign up for the Harlequin e-newsletter and download a free book from any series at

www.TryHarlequin.com